CW01660945

AQUAPHOBIA

A DCI Finnegan Yorkshire Crime Thriller - Prequel

Ely North

Red Handed Print

Copyright © 2022 by Ely North

All rights reserved. This book or parts thereof may not be reproduced in any form, distributed, stored in any retrieval system, or transmitted in any form by any means—electronic, mechanical, photocopy, recording, or otherwise—without prior written permission of the author, except in the case of brief quotations embodied in critical reviews and certain other non-commercial uses permitted by copyright law.

To contact ely@elynorthcrimefiction.com

Author's website at https://www.subscribepage.com/ely_north_home

https://www.facebook.com/elynorthcrimefictionUK

Disclaimer: This is a work of fiction. Names, characters, businesses, places, events, locales, and incidents are either the products of the author's imagination or used in a fictitious manner. Any resemblance to actual persons, living or dead, or actual events is purely coincidental.

Published by Red Handed Print

First Edition

Kindle e-book ISBN-13: 978-0-6452904-9-3

Paperback ISBN-13: 978-0-6452904-8-6

Prologue

William Wordsworth – The Force of Prayer or The Founding of Bolton Priory (1807)

This striding-place is called the STRID,
A name which it took of yore:
A thousand years hath it borne that name,
And shall a thousand more.
And hither is young Romilly come,
And what may now forbid
That he, perhaps for the hundredth time,
Shall bound across the STRID
He sprang in glee, for what cared he
That the river was strong, and the rocks were steep
But the greyhound in the leash hung back,
And checked him in his leap.
The Boy is in the arms of Wharf,
And strangled by a merciless force.
For never more was young Romilly seen
Till he rose a lifeless corpse.

1

Sunday 6th April 8:30 pm – Wharfedale, UK

The storm builds. A splinter of lightning stabs the night sky, splitting darkness into monochrome crazy paving. A laboured breath later, it's followed by a razor sharp crack of thunder. The repercussions rumble on, rolling over the countryside like a slow-moving battalion of Panzer tanks, growling, complaining. Everything living or dead vibrates to the sonic bass overture.

Something else builds.

It gathers momentum—covert, ominous, violent, unstopping—the power of water, ejected from the heavens in biblical proportions on the dales and fells of North Yorkshire.

It falls into the wide banks of the River Wharfe. Streams, brooks and becks explode into the primary artery, already swollen. A raging flow of frothing fury rushes downwards with escalating anger and mayhem.

Upstream, the river is wide and can carry the load, spilling excess into the surrounding fields and paddocks. The river is old and has witnessed this play a thousand times before.

Downstream, it's different.

Rugged limestone and millstone grit ambush the torrent into a narrow funnel called the Strid.

It has taken lives before.

Tonight, the Strid... will claim another.

2

Tuesday 8th April 9:45 am – Bolton Abbey

DCI Frank Finnegan and his young detective sergeant, Zac Stoker, stride briskly past the riverside tearooms.

Frank nods towards them. 'We'll stop on the way back and grab a cup of tea and a scone. Your shout,' he says with a chuckle.

'Hey, I got the last shout,' Zac replies, zipping up his waterproof jacket as the drizzle intensifies.

'It's true what they say about the Scots.'

'That's rich coming from a Yorkshire man,' Zac replies with a wry smile.

They duck under the police barrier tape, which stretches across the path and gateway. Frank glances at a small sign on a wooden post which reads—Strid Wood Nature Trail.

'Only a mile. Have you been here before?' Frank asks, looking up at his sergeant.

'Oh, aye. We always pay a visit at least once a year. Usually in the summer. My boys love messing about in the river.'

'It's a grand spot, that's for sure. My parents used to bring me and my brother here when we were children. My dad loved Bolton Abbey, so he did,' he adds wistfully as he stops for a moment to take in the scenery.

Gnarled oak trees hug the banks of the River Wharfe, surrounded by a carpet of vivid violet bluebells. The bell-shaped flowers hang their heads, as if ashamed of some terrible crime. Wild garlic permeates the air tempered by the earthy aroma of decaying leaf litter.

'Let's hope it's an accidental drowning,' Zac says. 'I don't want this place tainted by murder.'

'First reports indicated it was a young man, so I'm pretty certain it will be an accident. Probably got too close to the Strid and lost his footing. It doesn't matter how many bloody warning signs they erect; you always get some damn fool who knows better.'

'Aye, the invincibility of youth.'

'Although, if we suspect foul play, I reckon we could wangle a few days in Wharfedale. There's some friendly pub stays around these parts.'

'And fine ales.'

Frank laughs. 'Yep, and sumptuous pub grub to go with it.'

As they near the site of where the body was discovered in the river, they spot a small group of people ahead.

Paramedics, a police photographer, two uniformed officers, a couple of divers in wetsuits and a pair of hikers.

'Quite the gathering,' Frank says.

Zac stops dead in his tracks and grabs at Frank's arms.

'Oh, no,' he groans.

'What is it?'

'Guess who I just spotted?'

'Who?'

'Your favourite forensic pathologist.'

Frank's eyes bulge as his gaze falls upon the hulking frame kneeling next to a blue body bag.

'Bennett bloody Whipple,' he murmurs, almost in shock. 'What's he doing here? It's way out of his jurisdiction.'

'I think he does it for fun these days,' Zac replies.

They amble up to the assembly.

'Ah, Bennett, and how are you on this fine Yorkshire morning?' Frank declares, trying to sound cheerful.

The doctor stops his inspection of the body and glances over his shoulder.

'Detective Chief Inspector Finnegan, do you do it on purpose?' he booms in his strong Nigerian accent.

'Do what?'

He pulls his colossal frame to its full imposing height and gazes down on Frank and Zac.

'Addressing me as though we were at a garden party. When working in a professional capacity, I think it not only decorous, but appropriate to abide by the correct categorisation of our respective duties.'

'Meaning?'

'It's Doctor Whipple, inspector, Doctor Whipple!'

Zac suppresses the urge to laugh.

'I beg your pardon, Bennett... ahem, Doctor Whipple. Please accept my apologies. So, what brings you so far west? I thought your dominion ended in the borough of Scarborough?'

Bennett growls slightly. 'I'm the locum for the resident forensic pathologist of this district. Apparently, he's on long service leave. However, I'm not here to discuss such trifles.'

'I see,' Frank says as he fixes his attention on the body bag. 'So, what have we got here then?'

'I can certainly furnish you with my preliminary critique of the deceased, but you must remember—at this stage, it is merely conjecture.'

Bennet Whipple bends down rather awkwardly and unzips the bag. The cold, lifeless body of a young man stares up at them.

'A male,' the doctor states officiously.

'You don't say,' Zac mutters, out of earshot.

'Aged between late teens and mid-twenties.'

'How long has he been in the water?' Frank asks.

'I'd say not more than forty-eight hours, but longer than twenty-four. There is mild bloating, vascular marbling, and slight skin discolouration, but putrefaction is limited. Of course, that could be to do with the temperature of the water.'

'Any obvious injuries?'

'A cursory examination of the cadaver indicates no life-threatening injuries. Slight contusion to the right temple, some superficial grazing to the fingertips. A full post-mortem will postulate more factual analysis.'

'So, we're looking at a drowning,' Zac mutters, deep in thought.

'And what brings you to that conclusion, Sergeant Stoker!' Doctor Whipple roars.

'A dead body in the river?'

He sighs. 'I suppose it's in your nature to speculate based upon tenuous, rudimentary, substantiation, but sergeant, you have already ruled out the possibility of gross intoxication, poisoning, heart failure, seizure, and a myriad of other possibilities. That's the difference between our noble professions. One is grounded in cold, hard science, the other in wild flights of the imagination.'

'I'll bet you fifty quid he drowned,' Zac smirks, holding out his gambler's hand.

Doctor Whipple stares at the appendage with obvious disdain.

'Gambling is a disease of the mind which leads to the downfall of morality and, eventually, the body. However, there is one more thing I've deduced from my formative examination.'

'And what's that?' Frank asks.

'This young man was racist.'

Frank and Zac exchange glances.

'What leads you to that conclusion?' Frank enquires.

Doctor Whipple pulls at the body bag, exposing the shoulders.

'Here, on the deltoid muscle of the upper humerus, there's a tattoo. It reads—Whites Rule.'

The two detectives stare at the artwork of a white rose sitting above the wording. They both chuckle.

'I find neither the loss of human life, nor racism amusing—inspector.'

Frank rubs at his chin. 'It doesn't make him a racist, doctor. He was a Leeds United fan. The white rose is in their emblem, signifying Yorkshire. And—The Whites—is one of their nicknames.'

'A football team?' the doctor queries.

'So some believe. But it's only a rumour,' Zac says, drily.

'Oi, watch it sunshine,' Frank says with a grin as he points a finger at Zac.

'I find all sports to be an aberration of the human condition,' Doctor Whipple says, rising to his feet. 'The undertaker is on his way. I've finished with the body for now. You may instruct the paramedics to convey the cadaver back to the tearooms by stretcher. My secretary will inform you of the date and time of the post-mortem, inspector. Have an agreeable day.'

Frank and Zac watch with mild amusement as the great man plods heavily away.

'Barrel of laughs,' Frank mutters.

'I think he's in the wrong profession.'

'How'd you mean?'

'He should have been a children's entertainer.'

Frank chuckles before glancing down at the body. He stiffens and shakes his head, becoming serious as he drops to his knees.

'What happened to you, young lad?' he whispers. 'Your whole life ahead of you and a big wide world to explore and now it's gone, and you can't ever get it back.'

He rises and sighs.

'What a waste,' Zac says as he pats Frank on the shoulder.

'Aye, a bloody waste. Right, come on, let's find out what happened to this young chap.'

3

Zac places the tray down on the table as Frank studies his own notes.

'Twenty minutes and they're closing,' Zac says. 'No visitors today, or possibly tomorrow, what with everything cordoned off.'

'They're not bloody closing!' Frank replies. 'There'll be over thirty bodies on the ground in an hour's time conducting a search and they'll all need sustenance. Speak to the manager once we've finished our tea and scones. We'll need a boatload of sandwiches and snacks. Right, what have you got?'

Zac takes a seat, has a sip of his strong black coffee, then opens his notebook.

'Mr and Mrs Rogers from Doncaster are walking the Dales Way. They set off from Burnsall at seven-thirty this morning. Ambled along the trail, stopped at the Strid for a quick cuppa from a flask about nine, then carried on their merry way. About two hundred yards further on,

Mrs Rogers spotted something in the river as she was taking a pee in the bushes. At first, she thought it was a mannequin—why she'd assume that is anyone's guess.'

'Hope,' Frank replies as he bites into his scone topped with strawberry jam and clotted cream.

'She called her husband, who had a pair of binoculars—he's a Twitcher. He realised it was a dead body. They rushed to the tearooms and raised the alarm.'

Frank wipes the corner of his mouth on a serviette, then flicks open his notes.

'The divers said the young man's left foot was snagged between the fork of a submerged tree branch. The river's elevated because of the recent rainfall. According to the sergeant from Skipton, there was a huge thunderstorm on Sunday evening. It dropped five inches in the space of twenty minutes. Which means an hour later the river would have been a raging torrent.'

Zac stirs his coffee. 'It seems pretty straightforward, Frank. It was unusually warm on Sunday. The young lad goes for a refreshing dip, unaware a Tsunami is heading his way. When it hits, he's taken by surprise, is carried down the river and becomes snared on the branch.'

'Possibly. But where are his clothes?'

'If he left them on the bank near the water's edge, they'd have been swept away.'

'And how did he get here? I had a quick word with the estate manager. There are three car parks; one for the abbey, one for the Strid tearooms up top, and the riverside one where we parked. The car parks open at nine and close at seven, and there are no abandoned vehicles.'

'Maybe he was a hiker, or possibly he came by bus and intended to leave the same way?'

Frank finishes his scone and rubs his hands together. 'Let's look at what Whipple said. Although he's a bombastic prig, and a royal pain in the backside, he's bloody good at his job and his guesstimates are usually on the money.' He glances at his wristwatch. 'It's nearly twelve, Tuesday, which means the body entered the water between midday Sunday and midday Monday. After the thunderstorm on Sunday evening, no one in their right mind would have gone for a swim in a swollen river.'

'Which leads back to my original theory. He's hiking along, hot and tired. Goes for a dip, then bang! The water flowing down from the hills hits the Strid. That rock formation is a bottleneck, making the river far more dangerous. Of course, there is another possibility.'

'He took his own life?'

'Yes.'

'I've dealt with a lot of suicides over the years, and God only knows what unfathomable pain and anguish people must go through to end their lives, but why would he take his clothes off first?'

'Who knows what goes on in people's heads? Frank, you're not suggesting anything else other than accidental death or suicide, are you?'

Frank sips on his tea, then tuts. 'Come on lad, what's our ABC?'

Zac rolls his eyes. 'Assume nothing. Believe no one. Check everything,' he repeats with little enthusiasm.

'And Finnegan's Law?'

'Treat every death as murder until proven otherwise.'

'Good. Right, when the search party arrives, split them into two teams. One party to search upstream as far as Burnsall, the other to scour downstream as far as Addingham. Let's see if we can find his clothes.'

'That's a fair distance to cover.'

'It can't be helped. It is what it is.'

'Yes, boss.'

Frank stands up and pushes his chair under the table. 'You have a word with the manager about keeping the tearoom open and I'll see you outside.'

Frank fastens his jacket as he steps out into the grey daylight, heavy with pedestrian clouds. A cool breeze has an edge to it as intermittent mizzle continues to fall.

'Chief inspector!' a voice calls out.

Frank turns to witness the sergeant from Skipton striding down the nature trail. He breaks into an old man's jog, which is only slightly faster than walking pace.

'I'm glad I caught you. We've got an ID on the body, sir,' he says, panting a little.

'From whom?'

'A couple of extra constables have arrived on the scene. One of them recognised the deceased from the police photographs. She used to go to school with him.'

'Is she one hundred per cent certain?'

'Yes. Absolute definite.' He pulls out his notebook. 'His name is Luke Bretton, twenty-five years old. The PC and he were in the same year at school. He's a local from Skipton. She said she occasionally saw him around town. They weren't friends, but they'd nod their acknowledgements to each other.'

'Does she know where he lives?'

'No sir. But I ran his details through the PNC. He received a penalty notice when he was nineteen for shoplifting. Nicked a set of headphones. Fined eighty-quid, which was paid the same day by the mother—Eileen Bretton. Other than that, he's clean. Last known address was 16 Daleside Street, Skipton.'

'Anything else?'

'The constable believes Luke's biological father passed away some time ago.'

'Okay, excellent work, sergeant. That will save us some leg work. And don't forget to give your constable a pat on the back.'

'Will do.' The sergeant smiles as he walks off.

4

Frank knocks on the door. As he waits, he takes in his surroundings. The weathered stone house is in the middle of a long row of other terraces. He's bemused by the facades. They are all identical. The stone entrance and window openings are painted black. The door and window frames, all white. Net curtains protect inside from invasive eyes.

'Bit bloody odd,' he mumbles to Zac. 'It's like Legoland.'

Zac does a quick three-sixty as Frank knocks again. 'Yeah, not much originality.'

The door creaks open as a young woman's face peers through the crack, seeming a little apprehensive.

'Yes?'

He flashes his warrant card. 'Morning, miss. DCI Finnegan, North Yorkshire Police and this is DS Stoker. I'm looking for a Mrs Eileen Bretton. I believe she may live at this address.'

Concern spreads across the woman's face. 'Yes, she does, or at least she did. What's this about?'

'May we come in?' Frank asks, having already spotted a dozen pairs of net curtains twitching.

The woman reluctantly pulls the door fully open as Frank and Zac wipe their feet on a mat and make their way into a small living room.

'Why do you want to speak to my mother?' the woman says, holding an arm towards a leather couch. Frank and Zac take a seat.

'Are you Eileen's daughter?' Frank says with a fatherly smile.

'Yes.'

'What's your name?' Zac asks as he pulls out his notebook.

'Katy.'

'That's a nice name,' Zac says as he writes. 'Katy Bretton,' he repeats.

'No. It's Katy Kennedy, not Bretton.'

'Oh, I see,' Zac says with an element of surprise as he rectifies his mistake.

'You inferred your mother used to live here but not anymore?' Frank quizzes. 'Can you tell me where she's living now?'

Katy slumps into a chair and briefly places her head in her hands.

'Burnley Hospice.'

Frank and Zac exchange a concerned glance. Their task of informing a parent their child is dead just got a damn sight harder.

'I'm sorry to hear that,' Frank says, shifting uncomfortably. 'How long has she…'

'Two weeks, possibly a month. Pancreatic cancer. Look, is this about Luke?'

'Yes, it is,' Frank says in a whisper. 'I'm afraid I have some bad news. Your brother was found this morning, unresponsive in the River Wharfe downstream of the Strid.'

Zac rubs the top of his pen across his cheek nervously.

Her forehead creases in mild confusion. 'Oh,' is all she says without emotion. 'He's not my brother. He's my stepbrother,' she adds rather coldly.

Frank edges forward on the couch. 'I'm led to believe Luke's father is no longer alive?'

'That's right.'

'I see. We normally ask the next of kin to formally identify the body, but in the circumstances…' Frank trails off.

'And as Luke's father passed away some years ago…' Zac adds.

'You want me to do it?' Katy states, pre-empting the request.

***

Zac places the tray of tea and biscuits on a side table and hands out the refreshments.

'We need to ask you a few questions about Luke,' Frank begins. 'Did Luke live here?'

'Yes.'

'With you and your mother?'

'Yes.'

'When was the last time you saw him?'

'Sunday about midday. He went out not long after and I haven't seen him since.'

'The Sunday just gone?'

She nods.

'Can you describe what he was wearing?'

She points at a photograph above the fireplace. 'Same gear as he's got on in the photo. Light blue Adidas hoody, faded denim Levi's, a pair of Converse trainers.'

Zac picks up the photo and studies it before handing it to Frank.

'Converse All Stars, boss. Chuck Taylor.'

'Who the hell is Chuck Taylor when he's at home?' Frank says, scrutinising the image of Luke.

'He was an American basketball star from last century. He helped develop the modern basketball footwear.'

'You're very knowledgeable about these things, sergeant.'

'My lads have both got a pair. They're in vogue at the moment.'

'I see. He was a good-looking young man,' Frank says as he stares at the relaxed figure sporting a mischievous grin below the blue hoody.

'On the outside only.'

'What do you mean? Was he prone to violence, have a temper on him?'

'God, no! He was as soft as.'

'Do you mind if we borrow the photo? We'll return it once we've finished with it.'

'Take it and don't bother returning it. Mam won't be coming back here again.'

'We'll return it, just the same. Can you describe his mood on Sunday?'

She sighs and leans forward, hands clasped. 'He was agitated, as usual.'

Frank sips from his cup as Zac scribbles notes. 'Why was he agitated?'

'Same reason as always—his horses didn't win.'

Frank narrows his eyes. 'Horses? A bit early to be having a flutter.'

'He was a compulsive gambler, inspector. In fact, if I'm honest with you, he was a fucking nightmare. He moved back home from London two years ago and that's when it all turned to shit.'

'What happened?'

'He was forever in debt. There was always someone chasing him for money he'd borrowed. Mam kept bailing him out until all her savings were gone. She tried to get him help, counselling, but he wouldn't hear of it. He was always praying for the one big win that would help him repay all his debts. Then he was going to give up. Ha! Pigs might fly.'

'Do you know how much he was in debt and to whom?'

'He was in debt to everyone. I dread to think how much he owed,' she sneers.

'I take it you two weren't close?'

'Well spotted, inspector. I hated him. Everything was ticking along smoothly until he returned home, and then mam was diagnosed with cancer.'

Zac clears his throat. 'Was he the outside type—you know, walking, hiking, swimming?'

'Luke! You've got to be joking... unless you count going to the racetrack or dogs. He had two things in his life: gambling and video games. He was a loser.'

'What about mates, girlfriends?'

'Nah. He had one mate from his schooldays he used to hang out with when he first returned, but it didn't last long before they fell out.'

'And who was that?'

'Dane King.'

'Do you know why they had a falling out?'

'He never said, but I assume he'd borrowed money from him and never repaid it or stole from him.'

'Stole?'

'Yes. He stole from me, from mam. He landed a decent job when he came back, working at an antique shop. Lasted about a year before he got the sack and had been on the dole ever since. Like I said, a loser.'

'Did he suffer from depression or anxiety?'

'No. The only time he stressed was waiting for the racing results or when the loan shark came looking for him.'

'Do you know who the loan shark is?'

She scrunches up her face. 'Don't know the first name but I think his last name was... Grady... no, Brady. Ugly looking brute. Luke would hide behind the settee when he came knocking. Used to get me and mam to fob him off with some cock and bull story.'

'Did you ever witness this Brady fella threaten Luke?'

'Not really. He once said something like—you've got until next week or else, but I don't think he meant it as a threat. It was more like exasperation.'

'Did Luke do drugs, drink to excess, have any medical conditions?'

'No. He wouldn't waste money on drink and drugs when he could put it on a horse. And he had nothing wrong with him as far as I know.'

'Have you any idea what Luke would be doing at Bolton Abbey last Sunday or Monday?'

She shakes her head. 'No, not unless they were holding a donkey derby.' Her expression changes from one of weary anger to surprise. 'Hang on a moment... I thought you said he'd drowned? Why all these questions—you don't suspect someone did him in, do you?'

'We never said he'd drowned,' Zac explains gently. 'He was found in the water. He may have been dead before then. Until we receive the pathologist's report, we can't be certain as to the cause of death.'

'We're simply exploring all possibilities at the moment.' Frank nods to Zac and raises his eyes toward the ceiling.

'Katy, do you mind if I have a quick look around Luke's bedroom?' Zac asks.

'Go for it. Top of the stairs turn right. His room overlooks the back garden.'

As Zac makes his way upstairs, Frank continues his probing. 'Apart from Brady, can you think of anyone else who may have wanted Luke to come to harm?'

She snorts derisively. 'It would be easier to find people who didn't. Like I said, he begged, borrowed, or stole from anyone he knew. Christ, how am I going to tell mam,' she adds in a whisper as the full enormity of the situation bears down on her.

'Were your mother and Luke close?'

'Yes. She was well aware of all his faults, but she still loved him.'

'As mothers are wont to do,' Frank says with a wistful air. 'Do you mind me asking who and where your father is?'

She shrugs. 'His name is Carl Kennedy, and I don't know where he is and don't care. Another loser. Buggered off when I was twelve. Never seen him since.'

'It seems to me your mother has done all the heavy lifting in the family.'

'Yes. She's an angel,' she swallows, trying to hold back the emotion. 'And now she has a few weeks of misery left. The world's so unfair.'

Frank leans over and pats her on the arm. 'It is unfair. There's no two ways about it,' he murmurs softly. 'The only thing you can do is live the best life you can. Easy to say in trying times. But don't let the bad blot out the good.'

She nods and noisily blows into a paper tissue as Frank studies the ring finger of her left hand.

Zac reappears. 'All done upstairs, boss.'

Frank nods. 'Where does the animosity towards your stepbrother stem from?'

'When mam remarried, Luke resented it. We never got on. When he returned from London, mam had already been diagnosed. She tried all the usual treatments, which is bloody hard enough, but she also had to deal with his gambling, bailing him out. It was an enormous strain on her. I think the stress of it all has shortened her life.'

'I see. Well, thank you for your time, Katy. We'll be in touch to let you know about viewing Luke's body.'

'Will it be today?' she says as she leads them to the front door.

'Yes. We'll have an officer escort you. When do you intend to break the news to your mother?'

She shakes her head. 'I don't know. I'm not even sure if I should tell her.'

Frank and Zac exchange worried frowns.

'I think it's the right thing to do. And as soon as possible,' Frank offers softly. 'You wouldn't want her to hear about Luke's death from someone else or on the news.'

'No... no, of course not. I'm not thinking straight.'

'Perfectly understandable,' Frank says as he pulls at the door. 'You don't have an address for Luke's ex-friend, Dane King, do you?'

'I don't know where he lives, but he's a mechanic at Car Doctors near the railway station at the side of the canal.'

'And the name of the antique shop Luke worked at?'

'The Treasure Chest off Otley Road.'

'Thanks. You've been very helpful.' Frank hovers on the front step. 'Nice tidy place you've got here.'

'Thanks.'

'Does your mother own it or is it a rental?'

'Mam owns it. Still got a mortgage to pay for another couple of years, though.'

***

As the car pulls away, Frank turns to Zac.

'Anything useful in his bedroom?'

'Not really. Video games, clothes. Pretty sparse really.'

'No laptop or desktop?'

'No. He probably flogged them to fund his habit. Oh, I found this which is a bit peculiar,' he adds as he pulls a business card from his pocket whilst navigating a tight bend.

Frank studies the card and reads it out. 'Elliot Shackleton. Your Local Councillor, Town Mayor. Hmm... what would a young, unemployed, gambling addict want with the local mayor?'

'That's what I thought. Worth paying him a visit?'

'Yes, it is. We've got some ground to cover. It will be quicker if we split up. Drop me back at the station and I'll take a pool car and visit Mr Shackleton. You question Dane King. I'll meet you back at the station. If you arrive back before me, see if you can get a lead on this loan shark—Brady.'

'Will do. So what do you make of Katy?' Zac asks.

'Not much love lost between her and her stepbrother. How much would you say the house is worth?'

'Four bedroom terrace in a pleasant area—oh, two-fifty to three hundred grand.'

'Aye, I reckon the same. People have been murdered for far less. And her share in the property has just doubled.'

5

Zac finishes his sausage roll and swills it down with a gulp of bitter coffee. He stares through the windscreen at a narrowboat gently cruising along the canal as it heads out of town.

'Now there's a lifestyle. Nothing to do and all day to do it in. Maybe one day, many years from now,' he murmurs as he exits the car, locks up and walks across the road to the mechanics.

The workshop is a newish structure, and everything appears tidy, well maintained. He bypasses reception and heads towards the four large vehicle bays where he can see activity. As he enters, an older man with an unkempt beard calls out to him.

'Sorry mate, you're not allowed in here. Health and safety regs and all that.'

Zac brandishes his card. 'DS Stoker, North Yorkshire Police. I'm after Dane King?'

'What for?' the man asks suspiciously.

'I've a few questions for him.'

'Is he wanted?'

Zac ignores his question. 'Is he here?'

'Oi, Dane! There's a copper out here wanting a word with you,' he bellows.

A young, tall man appears from behind a car and saunters over.

'You Dane King?'

The young man hesitates. 'Yes. What's this about?'

Zac saunters outside, out of earshot of the older guy and Dane follows him.

'I'm afraid I have some sad news. An old friend of yours was pulled out of the River Wharfe near Bolton Abbey this morning—Luke Bretton.'

Dane's eyes bulge as he takes a step back and lowers himself down onto a stack of old tyres.

'Fuck,' he whispers, staring at the ground. 'Drowned?'

'We're not sure yet.'

'And he's definitely dead?'

'Yes, we're certain.'

'But... how?'

'That's what we aim to find out. Was it an accident, or suicide?'

'I'll tell you one thing—it won't have been suicide, not Luke.'

'Why do you say that?'

'Because he wasn't the type to get down about things, not while there's another race to bet on.'

'When was the last time you saw him?'

'Friday.'

'I heard you two had a falling out?'

Dane regains his composure and stands up. 'Who told you that? His stepsister?'

'Is it true?'

'Yeah, it's true. About a year ago, the prick.'

'What happened?'

'I beat the crap out of him. No point denying it. You'd have found out, eventually.'

'Why did you beat him up?'

He pulls a packet of cigarettes out of his side pocket and sparks up, inhaling deeply.

'Because I caught him fucking my fiancé.' Tears well in his eyes. 'The two people I loved the most did the dirty on me. We were due to get married. I'd left my mobile phone at home so nipped back at dinnertime to pick it up, and they were both at it hammer and tongs, in the kitchen of all places. Bastards, the pair of them.'

Zac coughs. 'You didn't patch it up with your girlfriend?'

He takes another drag on his smoke. 'Like hell! A leopard can't change its spots. Completely fucked my life up.'

'Did he owe you any money?'

He chuckles. 'Luke owed everyone money. I tried to persuade him to join Gamblers Anonymous, but he wouldn't hear of it. Said he didn't have a problem, and he was having a run of bad luck. It was simply a matter of time before he hit the jackpot. He liked to bet trebles and accumulators on long shots. Fucking mugs game.'

'When was the last time you spoke with him?'

'The day I gave him a belting.'

'But you said you saw him on Friday?'

'It's a small town, sergeant. I was driving past the bookies and saw him coming out of the doorway, all smiles. He'd obviously had a win.'

'Can you think of anyone in particular who'd want to harm him?'

'I dunno. Him and his stepsister never got on. And if you're thinking I had anything to do with his death, you can think again. I wouldn't jeopardise my future on that tosser.'

'So you're not sad to see him go then?'

'I don't know what I'm feeling at the moment,' he reflects as he drops his ciggy to the ground and grinds it into the gravel with his heel.

'Have you any idea what Luke may have been doing at Bolton Abbey on Sunday?'

He screws his face up. 'Nah, that wasn't his scene at all. If you'd told me he'd been murdered at the races, that I could understand.'

'I never mentioned anything about murder.'

'You wouldn't be asking all these questions if you didn't suspect foul play. Are we done?'

'Yes. For the moment. By the way, your ex-fiancé, is she still around?'

'No, she hot-footed it back down to Brighton with her tail between her legs the day after I caught Luke with *his* tail between her legs. Not seen her since and I hope I never see her again.'

'Okay Dane. Thanks for your time.'

'The pleasure was all yours,' he replies sullenly as he heads back into the workshop.

6

Frank couldn't find Elliot Shackleton at the town hall but got his home address and gleaned some useful information about him from a secretary. Driving ten miles southwest of Skipton, into the enemy territory of Lancashire, he arrives at Uplands Manor, a magnificent nineteenth century, ten bedroom stone house, swathed by exquisitely manicured formal gardens. A converted coach house and an elevated summer room and spa overlook the nearby Yorkshire Dales.

As Frank's rather grubby car crunches up the gravel driveway, he sighs in disbelief.

'Hell's bells, how the other half live. I'm in the wrong bloody job.'

Exiting the car, he takes in the crisp, fresh air, and marvels at the outstanding beauty of Mother Nature and the handiwork of man. As he strolls casually to the front entrance, a pungent whiff of smoke assaults his nostrils. In the garden to the left of the house, he spots a smouldering pile of grass clippings. Smoke drifts lazily into the air.

Momentarily, he's taken back to his childhood, raking grass from the front lawn as his father throws it onto a fire.

He climbs a set of stone steps and presses a buzzer. A peal of old-fashioned bells is followed by the click, click, click of sharp heels on hard tiles.

'Yes?'

An extremely attractive woman stands before him. Mid-thirties, high cheekbones, glossy black hair tied in a tight ponytail, elegantly dressed. For a moment, manners are forgotten as he gazes at perfection personified.

'Ahem, DCI Frank Finnegan, North Yorkshire CID,' he eventually says holding his card up for inspection

'How can I be of assistance?' the woman replies curtly.

'I'm here to see Elliot Shackleton. Is he your husband?'

'Yes, that's right. I'm Loretta Shackleton. Please come in, inspector.'

She chaperones him into the hallway and closes the door.

'May I enquire what this is about?'

Frank offers her a smile, which indicates—no.

'I see. Nothing serious, I hope. Although, the CID wouldn't be calling about an unpaid parking fine, would they? Follow me.'

She leads him into a snug and tastefully designed study, and points at a chair in front of a large leather-bound desk.

'Please take a seat. I shall inform my husband of your visit. He's presently on the line with a rather important call. May I offer you refreshments, tea, coffee, mineral water?'

'A cup of tea would go down a treat. White, two sugars, thanks.'

'My pleasure.'

She swishes from the room, leaving an enchanting scent in her wake.

'Her husband has fallen arse backwards into the butter,' he murmurs to himself. 'Although, never judge a book by the cover.'

He gazes out of the window at the plethora of greenery daubed with the occasional splash of vibrant colour. Fen violets nuzzle up against cotoneasters, their creamy white flowers offset against blood-red berries. Water parsnips sway lazily in the caress of a tender breeze at the side of a pond. Tall, rangy field elms duel with beech trees as laburnums watch on, their pendulous buttery blossoms like the sad doleful eyes of a puppy, belying their poisonous nature. Frank's mind wanders to his own allotment back in Whitby. Spring and autumn are his busiest time; sowing, thinning, fertilising, harvesting. He thinks of his wife, Meera, as a pang of melancholy washes over him. He hates being away from her but realises unless a suicide note turns up or an eyewitness offers vital information, he could be absent for most of the week.

Footsteps snap him back into reality as Loretta Shackleton bustles through the door carrying a tray containing cups, teapot, sugar bowl, a plate of biscuits and a dainty jug of milk.

'I apologise for the delay, inspector. My husband will be with you shortly,' she explains as she places the tray on the desk.

'There's no rush,' he replies, enjoying his surroundings.

She smiles at him, outwardly a pleasant smile, but behind twinkling emerald eyes there's keen intelligence at work, picking at threads.

'Magnificent gardens you have, Mrs Shackleton.'

'Thank you. It's a lot of arduous work to maintain, but it's worth it.'

'Do you do all the work yourself?'

'Good heavens no! We employ a full-time gardener, although he's on holiday at the moment. I'll leave you to pour your own tea,' she says as she departs once more.

Frank studies the assortment of biscuits. 'Ooh, Bourbons, my favourite,' he murmurs to himself as he takes one and bites into it.

As he chews, he surveys the room. On the desk is a recent photograph of Mr and Mrs Shackleton, all smiles for the camera, dressed to the nines in their finery. In the background are white marquees and elegantly decorated tables with three-tier sandwich plates loaded up. Another framed photo on a sideboard shows Elliot Shackleton shaking hands with the prime minister. There are no photos of children. He carefully pours the tea, drops two sugars into it and tops it up with milk. Footsteps resonate from the hallway as he quickly takes a gulp from the cup.

'Hell, that's a damn fine brew,' he says to himself.

'Ah, inspector Finnegan, my sincerest apologies for the delay. I was on the phone with the PM's secretary.'

Frank stands and shakes the outstretched hand. Elliot Shackleton is at least ten years older than his wife, but a handsome man, with a dark thatch of slicked back hair divided by a sharp side parting. A crisp white shirt sits beneath a smart black waistcoat. His scent is fresh, clean, with an underlying aroma of cedarwood. He exudes confidence, potential, and wealth.

'I see my wife has provided refreshments. I'd be lost without her,' he says as he pours himself a cup of black tea, refraining from the biscuits. Placing the cup and saucer on the desk, he takes up his seat.

'It's a while since I had a brew made with tea-leaves,' Frank notes as he helps himself to a Garibaldi and dunks it in his cup.

'Loretta is very particular about many things, tea being one of them. It must only be drunk from the finest bone china. Has to be brewed for five minutes exactly, and the milk always goes in last,' he says with a chuckle.

'We all have our quirks.'

'Indeed we do, inspector. Now, how can I assist you?'

'We're investigating the death of a young man at Bolton Abbey.'

'Ah, yes. Terrible business. I heard he'd drowned?'

'And where did you hear that? We've only recently informed the family.'

'Whispering leaves. There are a lot of tight-knit communities around these parts and gossip travels quickly. Do you have a name for this unfortunate young man?'

'Luke Bretton, a resident of Skipton. Twenty-five years old.'

Elliot relaxes back into his chair and takes a sip from his cup. 'I'm afraid the name doesn't ring any bells,' he says, appearing deep in thought.

Frank pulls out the photo and places it in front of him. Elliot picks it up and analyses the image, slowly shaking his head.

'You don't recognise him?' Frank asks.

'I'm afraid I don't, inspector.'

Loretta pops her head through the doorway.

'Pardon me for interrupting, gents.' Both men look at her. 'Elliot, I'm on my way out now to clean the car and pick up some shopping from Skipton. I'll be back in about two hours. Don't forget you have the council meeting tonight. You need to be prepared.'

'Yes, darling.'

'Pleased to meet you, inspector.'

'Likewise,' Frank says rising to his feet as she disappears. He sits down again as Elliot pushes the photograph back across the desk.

'I'm not much help to you,' he offers apologetically. 'Although, I am intrigued why you came to see me.'

Frank extracts the business card and hands it to him.

'We found your card in Luke's bedroom. On the back, it has a day and time pencilled in.'

Elliot flips it over. 'Hmm... Thursday, 3 pm, but no date.'

'It piqued my interest as to why a young unemployed man would have your council business card.'

'I'm not sure. I'd have to check my diary at council offices. My secretary makes all my appointments. Maybe Luke intended to see me over some matter. I have an open surgery every second Saturday from nine until twelve. But if it's a pressing matter, I try to be flexible. I am here to serve the people.'

Frank quickly finishes his tea and rises to his feet. 'Thank you for your time, Mr Shackleton. And if you could check your diary tonight and let me know if Luke's name crops up, I would be grateful. Here's my card. You can call me on my mobile any time.'

'Of course, inspector,' Elliot replies as he pushes back in his chair and escorts Frank out into the hallway. 'By your line of questioning, I deduce it's not an open and shut case of accidental drowning or suicide?'

'Too early to tell yet. Simply following procedure. I find it's better to be proactive. That way you're always one step ahead.'

'Yes, of course.'

'I hear you're standing for parliament at the next general election, Mr Shackleton?'

'Yes,' he says, followed by a loud laugh. 'It's the worst kept secret in the whole of North Yorkshire. Lord Bybrooke has served his constituency for over thirty years and has done a sterling job during some turbulent times. Now it's time for him to put his feet up and enjoy a well-deserved retirement.'

'Have you been pre-selected?'

'Not yet. However, I have been endorsed by the party hierarchy, so it's simply a matter of time before it's made official. You'll be pleased to know one platform I'll be running on is law and order,' he explains as he opens the front door.

'That's hardly new for the Tories. I read a speech the other day from a government minister. He was talking about introducing a bill in parliament proposing a league table for the country's police forces.'

'Yes. I think it's an excellent idea. With the rising crime rate, there needs to be accountability.'

Frank eyeballs him wearily. 'I suppose this league table will list the forces with the highest arrest rate, most convictions, worst crime rate?'

'Indeed. We believe transparency in these matters is essential to regain the public's trust.'

'The way to regain the public's trust and reduce the crime rate is to pay people a living wage, not naming and shaming police forces. League tables are for football teams, Mr Shackleton. Good day.'

7

The main bar at the Lion's Head public house is relatively quiet. A couple of hikers sitting in an alcove, two elderly farmers propping up the bar, and a pair of thirsty detectives.

'Here you go Frank,' Zac says, paying special attention not to spill a single drop of the precious fluid, as he places two glasses on the oak table. 'A pint of Timothy Taylor's dark ale for you, and a pint of Guinness for me. The bistro opens in thirty minutes. We'll get a couple in before then to whet the appetite.'

'Here's to a curious but interesting day,' he says holding his glass up. 'Cheers.'

'Cheers,' Zac replies as their glasses clink.

Silence descends as both men take long, joyful slugs of their beer.

'Sweet mother of Mary, I needed this,' Frank says.

'Aye, belter.'

Frank pulls his notebook out. 'Okay Zac, you can be the first one out of the gate. What have you got?'

'Dane King was refreshingly upfront. He fell out with Luke Bretton about a year ago when he caught him shagging his future wife. Gave him a belting and sent the girlfriend packing. He last saw Luke on Friday afternoon coming out of a bookies with a smile on his face but hasn't spoken to him since the incident with his ex. He's certainly still cut up about what happened and can obviously be prone to violence when pushed. I managed to trace the loan shark—Gareth Brady. His business is called—Cash On Demand. It seems to be legit. It's recorded with Companies House and he's VAT registered. He has an office above a bakers on Sheep Lane, just off the main drag in Skipton. I called around there, but no one was home. How'd you go with the town mayor?'

'Tried at the town hall first. He wasn't in but I obtained some useful intel from a secretary. Elliot Shackleton is a rising star. Only entered politics a few years back and is already mayor. He has friends in high places, apparently, and is being fast-tracked to enter parliament at the next election. One of the safest Conservative seats in the land, which means they're expecting remarkable things from him. Lives in a manor house on the other side of the border.'

Zac chuckles. 'I'm surprised they let you into Lancashire. Did you have to show your passport?'

'I've nothing against Lancashire. There's only one thing wrong with it.'

'Which is?'

'It's not Yorkshire. Anyway, Elliot Shackleton said he'd never heard of Luke. He said he was going to check his diary tonight. They've got some council meeting going on. I tell you what, though, his wife is easy on the eye. She's a real cracker. Although, I suspect she's a hard taskmaster,' he adds thoughtfully as he takes a slurp of ale.

'Oh, one other thing Dane King mentioned. He said Luke was not the type to take his own life, not while there was another horse to bet on.'

'Backs up what the stepsister said.'

'And he couldn't imagine what Luke would be doing at Bolton Abbey. Said it wasn't his scene.'

'So, we've questioned three people, two of whom don't care Luke's dead and one who denies he's ever heard of him. We also know Luke was not well liked because of his scant regard for other people's money.'

'And not the sort of person to go for a restorative walk along a riverbank, alone.'

'No, indeed not. What the hell was he doing there in the first place? Tomorrow we'll round this Brady fella up for a chat and pay a visit to the antique shop. I'm beginning to feel sorry for Luke Bretton,' Frank says as he shakes his head.

'Get real, Frank! The lad was a bloody rogue of the highest degree. Robbing and stealing from family and friends, and while his mother's fighting cancer. He's scum, and that's all there is to it.'

'He had an addiction, Zac. Put yourself in his shoes for a moment. Imagine forever fighting the urge to gamble and always losing the battle. He'd have experienced guilt for borrowing, cadging, stealing from his loved ones. It would have been a terrible burden to carry around. Yes, he was a bit of a rogue, but he was young, and needed help and got none. He didn't deserve to die.'

'I think he was the master of his own destiny. If you act the way Luke did, then eventually you're going to piss off the wrong person. You're going soft in your old age, Frank.'

'Possibly. Anyway, we're getting ahead of ourselves. I know I say treat every death as murder until proved otherwise, but this is looking increasingly like an accident. Come on, sup up. It's my shout, then I really must give Meera a call. Oi, and you make sure you call your missus and the kids, right?'

'Yes, Frank. And by the way, you're forgetting something.'

Frank picks up the empty glasses and shuffles from his seat. 'What?'

'The post-mortem early tomorrow morning... with Doctor Whipple?'

Frank groans. 'Sweet merciful shit-on-a-stick! There's never a dull moment, is there? I don't know what I did in a previous life to deserve this, but it must have been something pretty bad,' he mutters as he heads to the bar. 'You realise I'll have nightmares tonight—Whipple and a post-mortem. A marriage made in hell!'

8

Wednesday 9th April 7:35 am

Frank regrets ordering a full English breakfast and now wishes he'd followed Zac's example and stuck to toast and marmalade. He shuffles nervously as Doctor Whipple weighs the liver extracted from the cadaver.

'Standard weight for his height. 1561 grams,' the doctor notes, in his booming baritone voice.

'Any damage?' Frank asks.

Bennett Whipple eyes Frank wearily. 'No. A healthy liver with no sign of alcohol abuse or disease. Now for the genitalia,' he adds with relish as he picks up a scalpel.

Frank shoots Zac a distressed glance, then closes his eyes. A few moments elapse.

'Hmm... interesting,' Bennett murmurs.

Frank doubts it is interesting but asks, anyway. 'What's interesting?'

'The epididymis is empty.'

'The eppy diddy what muss?'

Bennett Whipple places his scalpel down and sighs. 'The epididymis, inspector, the epididymis!' he bellows.

Frank shrugs.

'Sperm is produced in the seminiferous tubules. Once the sperm has matured, it is transported via the seminiferous tubules to the epididymis where it awaits ejaculation,' he explains with restraint as he picks up his scalpel once more.

'A bit like waiting for a bus?' Frank asks.

He slams his scalpel back down. 'Do you deliberately try to antagonise me, inspector!' he roars.

'I think it comes naturally,' Zac offers with a weak smile.

'So let me get this right, doctor,' Frank begins, long ago immune to the eccentricities of Bennet Whipple. 'Are you saying he didn't have any lead in his pencil?'

Bennett stares at the ground and taps his foot, agitated. He readjusts his spectacles and glowers down at Frank.

'I'll try to put this in the most unsophisticated way I can, inspector, for your benefit. He was devoid of sperm. Being a healthy young man, with no obvious malfunctioning of the reproductive organs, the testes—to you—this leads me to one conclusion, he'd recently ejaculated before his demise.'

'How recently?'

'The full sperm reproduction cycle in a healthy male takes between sixty seven to seventy-seven days. However, sperm is produced continually, even within thirty minutes of ejaculation.'

'Hell, that's a quick turnaround. At my age, when I have sex these days, it takes me a week before I'm ready to go again,' Frank chuckles.

'Inspector Finnegan!' Doctor Whipple thunders.

'Sorry. So he had sex, fell into the water, and drowned?'

Bennett folds his arms, losing patience, which is wafer thin at the best of times.

'The term *drowning* is an archaic misnomer that belongs in the history books, inspector. Submersion or immersion in liquid results in respiratory impairment. When fluid is carried to the lungs, it interferes with the surfactant protecting the cells of the lung, which are responsible for exchanging oxygen. In other words, his lungs were full of water which caused the curtailment of the oxygen supply to the brain, leading ultimately to fibrillation of the heart causing a blood clot in the left atrium. This triggered a cardiac arrest.'

Frank scratches the back of his head. 'Hmm... I think for our intents and purposes we'll stick to the archaic term—drowned.'

Bennett Whipple clenches his fists, closes his eyes and takes a deep breath.

‘So did he die from a heart attack or from drowning?’ Frank questions thoughtfully, much to the chagrin of the doctor, who eyeballs him resignedly and rubs his hands together, trying to remain calm.

‘Impossible to tell. It could have happened simultaneously or at least within a few seconds of each other.’

‘Can you hazard an approximate time of death?’

‘As I initially indicated in my preliminary appraisal at the location of his demise, between twenty-four to forty-eight hours before the body was found. But that is an educated speculation.’

‘So between Sunday morning and Monday morning?’ Frank reiterates.

‘Yes.’

‘You couldn’t narrow it down a tad, could you?’

‘Inspector! I am a man of science. My work is based on facts and exhaustive scientific research. I refuse to indulge in parlour games! I have furnished you with my professional critique. Whether you wish to accredit any credence to it, is your choice! I cannot narrow it down further, but I can certainly, unequivocally, endow you with an undeniable truth!’

‘Go on,’ Frank replies, his interest piqued.

'This man died at some point between the last time he was seen alive and the first time he was seen dead. Does that help?'

'Not really. We're going backwards.'

Bennet Whipple pulls a handkerchief from his coat pocket and dabs at the sweat on his brow.

'May I continue my exploration of the cadaver, inspector?' he asks quietly.

'No problem, Bennett. We've learnt all we need to know. We'll leave you in peace,' Frank states as he pops a Polo mint into his mouth.

Bennett Whipple silently seethes at being addressed by his first name whilst in a working environment but says nothing as he scrutinises the detectives as they depart the mortuary.

'That man could test the patience of a saint,' he mumbles to himself as he picks up his scalpel and returns to his work with an unnatural zeal.

9

'That man could test the patience of a saint,' Frank says, as he fastens his seatbelt, then fires the engine.

'Aye. I wonder what his dinner parties are like?'

'A laugh a minute. Anyway, we're not much wiser than when we went in. Luke Bretton died of a heart attack or drowned—or both. We don't know why he was near the Strid, or how he ended up in the water. All we know is it would be out of character for him to be there... but it doesn't mean he was murdered, nor does it mean he wasn't murdered.'

'We do know a bit more,' Zac replies as Frank puts the car into gear and pulls away. 'We know he emptied his baw-bag shortly before he met his maker.'

Frank turns to him. 'You have a poetic way with words, sergeant. Scotland has produced a disproportionate number of poets compared to its population. You missed your calling in life.'

'Thanks, boss.'

'Pleasure. Okay, so Luke had sex immediately prior to death.'

'Not necessarily sex. He could have been masturbating, got over excited as he climaxed, lost his footing and taken a tumble.'

'If he were a sexual weirdo who liked to masturbate—naked—in the countryside, I'm sure his stepsister or ex-best mate would have mentioned it. At age twenty-five, he would have had some sort of police record; flashing, indecent exposure.'

'I suppose.'

'Which likely means he had sexual relations with another person at, or near, Bolton Abbey.'

'You're assuming Raspberry Whipple is correct,' Zac says.

'Has the good doctor ever been wrong before?'

'No. But there's a first time for everything.'

'True. But I doubt it... not with his unblemished record. A pain in the backside he may be, but he's at the top of his game. Right, onwards and upwards. Loan shark—Gareth Brady, here we come,' Frank says as he crunches gears.

Frank and Zac climb a set of grubby concrete steps to the first floor. A large, frosted glass frontage greets them.

Zac chuckles as he reads the signage etched into the glass. 'Cash On Demand – Cashflow Solutions Tailored To Your Needs.'

'It looks like loan sharks have gone all twenty-first century,' Frank says with a chuckle.

'Same shit, different bucket.'

Frank pushes open the door without knocking. They are instantly hit with the suffocating smell of thick cigarette smoke. Behind a desk is a bulky man, reading a sheet of paper, cigarette dangling from the corner of his mouth.

'Don't you know smoking kills? They even state it on the packet for the hard of understanding,' Frank says as he makes his way over to a window and pushes it open.

The man lazily puts the paper down. 'I wondered how long before you lot showed up,' he states in a deep, croaky voice, braised long in nicotine.

'Us lot?' Zac queries.

'Yeah, coppers. I can spot them a mile off. At least him I can,' he says, nodding at Frank. 'You look more like a failed contestant auditioning for a boy band.'

'Thanks,' Zac says with a grin.

'It wasn't a compliment.'

Frank grabs a swivel chair on wheels and pushes it to the front of the desk and takes a seat. He surveys the features of Gareth Brady. He has the head of a pit bull. A squashed nose splays out above thin lips, one cauliflower ear, and a scar below his left eye.

'DCI Finnegan and DS Stoker, by the way,' he says holding up his ID. 'You used to be a boxer.' Frank states.

Gareth stubs his ciggy into an overflowing ashtray and immediately sparks up a fresh one.

'Had my fair share of wins,' he replies, pushing back in his seat.

'And your fair share of losses, looking at the state of your mush. I used to do a bit of boxing myself in my younger days. What were you—a heavyweight?'

'Middleweight.'

'Hmm... You've stacked the weight on. How many fights?'

'Thirty seven, professional.'

'Wins?'

'Twenty. Got duped out of another five. The ref was bribed.'

'Of course he was.'

'As fascinating as this is, ask your questions, then piss off. I've got work to do.'

'When was the last time you saw Luke Bretton?'

'About a month back, the fucking little toerag. If I'd have got my hands on him, I'd have...' he trails off.

'You'd have what—killed him?' Zac asks as he leans up against a filing cabinet.

'I'd have given him a slap, that's all.'

'Is that what you call cash-flow solutions tailored to your needs?'

'He was taking the piss.'

'You have a conviction for assault and battery, Mr Brady. Like to throw your weight around, do you?' Frank queries.

'That was over twenty years ago.'

'You had a stint as a nightclub bouncer?'

'You've done your homework, who's a clever lad,' he replies with a sneer accompanied by a slow hand clap.

'You got a bit over excited in ejecting a young lad from a club.'

'He was a mouthy little shit and had a go at me. I gave him a light spanking.'

'He was taken to hospital with a broken jawbone and two missing teeth. Hardly a light spanking. Short fuse, have you?'

'I did my time, paid my penance to society and learnt my lesson.'

'How much did Luke Bretton owe you?' Frank continues.

'Five grand. Five grand I won't be getting back.'

'When did you first lend to him?'

'About a year ago. He wanted five hundred. He had a job then, seemed like a decent type. Didn't appear to be into the drugs. I thought he was a reasonable risk.'

'How does your business work?'

'Quite simple. People who have a temporary cash-flow problem come to me to help them out. If I think they're the type to pay me back, I lend them what they need.'

'With interest, of course?'

'Of course with fucking interest. This is a legitimate business, not a charity.'

'What are your rates?'

'If they pay back within a week, there's no charge. Then it goes up by ten per cent a week.'

Frank whistles. 'Bit steep. So if I borrowed a grand from you, after a month I'd owe you about thirteen hundred quid?'

'Thirteen hundred and thirty-one, to be precise.'

'Nice return on your investment, over thirty per cent in a month. But I suppose you have overheads; this office to run, transport and all the tax and VAT you have to pay.'

'Like I said, it's a legitimate business. Go check if you want.'

'We already have,' Zac says.

'If Luke borrowed five hundred from you, then how come he ended up owing you five grand?' Frank says as he drops a Polo mint into his mouth.

'He paid his initial loans back. Sometimes within the week, other times within a month. Then about three months back, he came to me for two thousand. That's when he started to give me the run-around.'

'So he didn't actually owe you five grand... only the two?'

'Tomorrow, why don't you call in to see your bank manager. Tell him you're only going to pay back what you borrowed for your mortgage, not the interest. See what he says.'

'We spoke with Luke's sister yesterday,' Zac begins. 'She said around six weeks ago you threatened him. You said he'd better pay up or else. Or else what?'

'I was trying to frighten him. Why would I kill him? That way, I'd never get my money back.'

'Who said he was murdered?' Frank asks.

'Don't come the smart Alec. It's all over town that he came to a sticky end. Any further questions?'

Frank rises and kicks the chair away with his foot, sending it rattling into a cupboard at the far end of the office. He drops his card on the desk.

'If you think of anything pertinent to our enquiries, please let me know.'

Gareth Brady chortles. 'Of course, chief inspector. I always like to help our boys in blue. They need all the fucking help they can get.'

Frank and Zac turn to leave. 'Oh, what type of car do you drive, Gareth?' Zac asks.

'Jaguar.'

'Of course you do. Silly question.'

'Mark II Auto. Nineteen-sixty-three model. Mint condition. She's my pride and joy.'

As Frank heads to the door, he points at the nicotine stained ceiling. 'Look at the state of that. Imagine what your lungs are like? If I were you, I wouldn't be making any long term holiday plans. Have a nice day.'

10

The tinkle of a bell rattles as they walk through the door of the antiques shop. A middle-aged man, slightly balding, with a wispy ginger thatch, looks up from behind the counter.

'Good afternoon gentlemen,' he offers in a soft, polite tone. 'Browsing?'

'Miles Brandon?' Frank says.

'Yes.'

Frank displays his warrant card and introduces himself and Zac.

'Ah, I see. You're here about Luke Bretton.'

'Yes. If you don't mind answering a few questions. Purely routine,' Frank says as Zac wanders around the shop inspecting artefacts.

Miles Brandon scurries to the door and flips the sign from open to closed then drops the latch.

'A terrible business. I've heard the rumours and I'm hoping they're not true. A death of such a young man is always tragic, but murder... Well, that's another level up.'

'How long did Luke work here, Mr Brandon?'

'A little over a year.'

'Was he a good worker?'

'Yes. I couldn't fault him... at first. He was punctual, polite, had the gift of the gab and was keen to learn.'

'So what happened—why did you sack him?'

Miles heaves a deep sigh and sits down on an ancient stool. 'I noticed the cash register was down, not regularly, but occasionally. I had another assistant working part-time, so I wasn't certain who was dipping their hand in the till.'

Frank stares up at the CCTV camera mounted at the back of the shop.

'Didn't the camera confirm the culprit?'

'No. It was baffling. And the money only disappeared when both Luke and the part-time assistant were working together.'

'Sneaky.'

'Indeed. I assumed it must be a sleight of hand, as the money was deposited into the till.'

'How much are we talking about?'

'Oh, small amounts; sometimes twenty, sometimes fifty pounds.'

'How did you catch him?'

'I didn't. One day, I confronted the pair and told them one of them was stealing. I said I was going out the back for five minutes and when I returned to the front of the shop, I expected the thief to have left. If they hadn't, then I'd have no other choice but to let them both go. When I returned—Luke was gone.'

'He had some scruples, then?'

He emits a wry laugh. 'Ha, yes. That's what I thought. He was a likeable lad, or so I thought. About a week later, I did a stocktake to make sure there was nothing missing.'

'Bit late in the day?'

'Yes. It was slack of me.'

'And?'

'Five or six items were unaccounted for; a china doll, a few rings, a Hitler Youth knife, an ashtray. Combined, they were probably worth about a thousand pounds at auction. But when I unlocked the watch cabinet, my prized possession was missing: a 1963 Omega Speedmaster watch. A beautiful item.'

'Timeless,' Zac says with a grin.

Miles nods, missing the bad joke. 'Yes. Very rare.'

'And what was its value?'

'A conservative estimate would be twenty-five.'

'Hundred?'

'Thousand.'

'Stone the crows! Did you report it to the police?'

'No. I paid Luke a visit and asked him to return the watch, but it was too late. He'd already sold it online to a private buyer. The damn fool only got four thousand for it. I told him I was going to the police, that way I could recoup the loss against my insurance. He begged and pleaded with me not to, but I was adamant. I had no other choice.'

Miles hesitates as Frank and Zac swap glances.

'But you didn't?' Zac prompts.

Miles shakes his head and averts his gaze, almost ashamed. 'No.'

'Why?'

'He threatened me.'

'Physically?'

'Ahem, no, he wouldn't hurt a fly—physically. He threatened to tell my wife.'

'About?'

He shuffles uncomfortably, and picks at his waistcoat. 'Our relationship,' Miles whispers, sad, mournful.

'A sexual relationship?' Frank asks.

He nods.

'So Luke was gay?'

'Sexuality is not always black and white, inspector.'

'He was bisexual?' Zac probes.

'Yes.'

'Did you pay him for sex?'

Miles squirms. 'I didn't *pay* him for sex. But I did give him money afterwards. He was always short of money even though I pay my staff well.'

'And when was the last time you saw him?' Frank asks.

'I used to see him around town occasionally. But the last time I saw him to speak to was the day I asked for the watch back.'

'Okay, well thanks for your time and candour, Mr Brandon,' Frank says, handing his card over. 'If you think of anything else—call me.'

Zac unlocks the door.

'You go ahead sergeant, I'm going to have a peruse and see if I can buy something nice for the missus,' Frank says.

'No worries. I'll grab a bite to eat and see you back at the car.'

Miles relaxes a little. 'Anything in particular you're after, inspector?'

'Not sure. How about earrings? Something elegant, understated.'

'What lady can resist earrings,' he says as he walks behind the counter and retrieves a leather case and opens it up, displaying a multitude of choices.

'Hell,' says Frank. 'Sometimes too much choice is a bad thing.'

His eyes dart over the contents and are drawn to a pair.

'Ah! I reckon she'd love these.'

'Excellent choice, sir. Retro silver, original Mikimoto cultured pearl earrings, circa 1940. Hallmarked with the makers' mark M and S.'

'Japanese?'

'Yes. The purest white. Quite breathtaking.'

'How much?'

'Two hundred and fifty pounds.'

'Strewth! That is breathtaking.'

'For you inspector, a ten per cent discount. You've got an eye for the finer things. I sold another pair of these a few weeks ago.'

'Popular then?'

'Not popular. They're extremely rare. The woman in question has exquisite taste and is one of my best customers. She's the mayor's wife,' he says as he removes the pearls from the case and places them in Frank's large palm.

'Loretta Shackleton?'

'Yes. Have you met her?'

'Briefly. Fine figure of a woman.'

'Indeed she is.'

'And did you give her a discount?'

Miles chuckles. 'No, I didn't. The Shackletons are not short of a bob or two.'

'No, so I gather. Okay, I'll take them.'

'I'll put them in their box and gift wrap it. I'm sure your wife will be delighted.'

'You don't know my wife. She can be contrary at the best of times, but I'd be nothing without her.'

11

Frank beams with satisfaction as the casserole dish is placed in front of him. He moves his pint slightly out of the way as he pulls the feast forwards.

'My favourite. Meat and tatty pie. Meera makes the best pie in the world, but I reckon this is a close second.'

The pastry emits a satisfying crunch as his knife slices into it. Zac pours the last of his Guinness down his throat and asks the waiter for two more pints. He takes a large bite of his burger and relaxes back in his chair.

'Oh, I needed this,' he says.

'I don't know where you put it. You must have hollow legs,' Frank says with a chuckle. 'You're built like a beanpole, but by God you can put the food away... and the ale.'

'I learned from the best,' he replies as Frank scoops a generous forkful of pie into his mouth.

As the two men enjoy their evening meal together, talking of football, their wives, Zac's children, eventually and inevitably, the conversation returns to the death of Luke Bretton.

Zac takes a slug of beer and smacks his lips as he pushes his empty plate away.

'For all intents and purposes, we've been treating this as a murder investigation,' he begins. 'But we're still no closer to finding out how he actually died. Accident, suicide, or murder.'

'Aye, it's a tough one. I called the estate manager at Bolton Abbey earlier and he reckons they had a hundred and twenty vehicles use the car parks on Sunday. If each car only contained two people, it's still two hundred and forty folk wandering around. Not to mention hikers walking the Dales Way.'

'Luke's photo is all over our social media sites, and the local news bulletins.'

'And not a single person has come forward to say they saw him. He's like Will-o'-the-wisp. Which leads me to believe he was there after dark on Sunday night.'

'But why? And was he alone?'

'And where are his clothes? We have no facts, so let's look at some probabilities. If you're going to take your own life, do you get undressed before you throw yourself in the water?'

'Probably not.'

'If the outdoor lifestyle is not your cup of tea, do you suddenly decide to take a stroll in the countryside?'

'No. It would be totally random.'

'That's right. People behave in patterns. They repeat things. So what do we know?'

'There are four people who had a good reason to do him in.'

'Let's go through the suspects and their motives,' Frank says as he pulls a pen from his jacket and grabs a paper napkin

'Dane King,' Zac begins.

'The ex-best friend—jealousy, anger, bitterness, eventually gets the better of him.'

'Katy Kennedy.'

'Greed. The bitter stepsister, set to inherit half of her mother's house when she passes. Why split it two ways with her stepbrother when she can have it all.'

'Gareth Brady.'

'Anger and a reputation to uphold. The ex-boxer, bouncer, turned loan shark, furious over losing his money, and loss of face. If he let Luke get away with not paying him back, then others might have thought they could get away with it too.'

'Miles Brandon.'

'Fear of his extra-marital activities being revealed to his wife. Swindled out of a hell of a lot of money, then threatened about his seedy private life. Who knows, maybe Luke was blackmailing him, and Miles met him on Sunday night to hand money over. All he had to do was lure him down to the Strid and push him in.'

'Naked?' Zac frowns.

'Maybe they had sex beforehand?'

Zac sips on his pint. 'Every one of them has a powerful motive. What about the mayor, Elliot Shackleton? Is he off the radar?'

'Not entirely. I spoke with him this morning. He said there was no entry in his diary to meet with Luke. But we only have his word for it.'

'So why would Luke have Elliot's business card with a day and time on it?'

'Exactly. It's not like they moved in the same circles.'

'I'm at a loss, Frank. It seems the more we uncover, the less we know.'

'Okay, tomorrow we begin round two. We quiz all four potential suspects again, and Elliot Shackleton. This time we ask for their alibis for Sunday night, and we check out every one of them. I'd also like to speak with Luke's mother, Eileen, but...'

'Hmm... a delicate situation.'

'I know, but she could hold the key. We'll need to tread carefully. You can run it by the daughter, Katy Kennedy, tomorrow. Get her blessing.'

'Why me!' Zac says, appalled at the suggestion.

'Why you? It's very simple, Zac—chain of command. I'm in charge. Now get the beer in and pick your jaw up off the table. One for the road, then I'm going to hit the hay, and I suggest you do the same. Tomorrow we won't be tightening the noose, but we'll certainly be erecting the scaffold.'

12

Thursday 10th April 8:25 am

Katy Kennedy doesn't receive the request well. Firstly surprised, her emotion soon morphs into anger.

'Don't you think she's been through enough?' she shouts at Zac.

'We wouldn't ask if we didn't think it important,' Zac explains, feeling like a heel.

'My God, the bastard is still making our lives a misery from beyond the grave.'

She slips back in her chair and drops her head into her hands.

'All we're asking is you pose the question to your mother. Ask if she's willing to give us a few minutes of her time.'

'Ha! The irony of it. Give you a few minutes of her time. How much time do you think she has to give?'

'I'm sure your mother would like us to solve this case before she...' He stops, unable to find the appropriate words.

'You can say it, you know. They're only words—they won't bite. Before she dies.'

Zac flushes and glances out of the window. 'There is a strong possibility Luke was murdered. Your mother would want to see justice for her only son. Don't you think the choice should be in her hands, not yours?'

'Don't try to guilt me. Anyway, you don't need my permission or mam's to question her.'

'No, we don't. We may be police, but we are still human. If we don't have yours and your mother's blessing, then we won't question her.'

She relents. 'Okay. I'm heading over there in an hour. I'll ask and let you know, although she won't tell you anything new.'

Zac smiles. 'Thanks,' he says softly. 'One last question. Can you tell me where you were on Sunday evening?'

'Oh, you suspect *me* now, do you?'

Zac is taking a passive-aggressive beating, but it's part of the job. 'The more people we eliminate from our enquiries, the better chance we have of finding a resolution.'

'I arrived at the hospice about three in the afternoon and left about ten at night. There's a register. You have to sign in and out.'

'What time did you arrive back home?'

'About ten-thirty. Made a hot chocolate and went to bed.'

'Did you drive or get a taxi?'

'I don't have a car. I took an Uber. The receipt is on my phone if you'd like to see it?'

She performs a few clicks on her mobile and passes it to him. He briefly studies it before he hands it back.

'Happy? Now, if you don't mind, I need a shower.'

'Of course. I can see myself out,' he replies as his detective brain whirs into gear.

13

Frank is soft-soaping the secretary at the town hall. All smiles and amiable chit-chat. It appears the mayor's secretary has taken a shine to the garrulous Frank.

'Yes, I spend a lot of time on my allotment. It's therapeutic, peaceful,' he says thoughtfully, leaning up against her desk.

'Sounds idyllic.'

'It's on top of the east cliff of Whitby, about a mile from the sea. It's beautiful whatever time of year—the salt air, the mournful cry of seagulls. During spring and summer, it's awash with insects and birds. Heavenly scents drift through the air. The distant sound of the unrelenting waves. During autumn, the colours, and shades slowly transform. And of course, I know all my produce is grown organically. Only natural fertilisers. Nurture the soil and Mother Nature takes care of the rest.'

'You make it sound so rugged and romantic. I'm going to tell my husband about it, hopefully it may inspire him. All he does in his spare time is watch the telly or go down the pub with his feckless mates.'

'I tell you what, the next time you're in Whitby, call me and I'd be delighted to show you my allotment. And my wife is a history buff. If there's anything about Whitby's history she doesn't know, then it's not worth knowing.' He hands her his card.

'That's very generous of you, Inspector Finnegan. I may take you up on that.'

'Make sure you do, and please, call me Frank. We could have a meal together—as couples, of course. Wouldn't want my wife getting the wrong idea,' he says with a nod and a wink.

She giggles like a besotted teenager despite being in her late forties.

He sighs and glances at his watch—deliberately. 'I can catch up with Mr Shackleton later. Shame he's not in, though. Would have saved me a lot of time.'

He makes to leave.

'Without prying, what exactly did you want to see Mr Shackleton about?'

'Oh, nothing much. A trifling matter. It's to do with the death of the young man at the Strid recently. Not that Mr Shackleton has anything to do with it—good Lord, no. I've heard on the grapevine he could be a future leader of this great nation of ours.'

'I believe it's only a matter of time. Once he's elected, which is already virtually guaranteed, I think he'll play out his first term, then make his move for the top job. He has a common touch, despite his wealth. And he's damned handsome and charismatic.'

'Aye, too true. Who needs good policies when you can woo the birds out of the trees?'

'My sentiments entirely,' she replies, missing Frank's well-hidden sarcasm. 'So, what was this trifling matter you were talking about—maybe I could help you out?'

'Oh, that's very kind of you, Margi.'

14

The palliative care nurse leads the way down the corridor. It's the first time Zac has visited a hospice, and he's thankful it's nothing like a hospital, which to him is organised chaos. The nurse stops outside a door and pauses.

'Please try to be as brief as possible. Eileen is exhausted today. You're her third visitor,' she explains in hushed tones.

'Who else has visited?' Zac asks.

'Her daughter early this morning. And her solicitor left about an hour ago. She's obviously on a lot of medication to manage the pain, so she might be a little groggy. If she falls asleep, please don't wake her. Is your mobile phone definitely on silent?'

Zac checks again. 'Yes.'

'Good.' The nurse gently knocks on the door and walks in. 'Eileen, I've a gentleman to see you. It's Detective Sergeant Stoker from North Yorkshire CID.'

Eileen is propped up in bed with her eyes closed. A tube runs from her upper arm to a syringe driver on a table next to her. Her breathing is laboured and noisy. The sight shocks Zac as a wave of pity sweeps over him. He didn't want to do this. It's not right.

'Eileen,' the nurse gently repeats.

Her eyes flicker open, accompanied by a thin smile.

'I'll leave you to it. Ten minutes—max,' the nurse whispers to Zac.

He nods as he takes up a seat next to the bed.

'You coppers get younger by the year. You're only just out of nappies,' Eileen says.

Zac grins. 'I'm on solids now, though.'

She chuckles. 'Scottish—what part?'

'Edinburgh.'

'I took the kids to the Edinburgh Tattoo one year. They seemed to enjoy it, but it was too noisy for me. All that banging and the screeching bagpipes. I found it quite nerve jangling.'

'Ah, the bagpipes. It is a divisive instrument. People either love them or hate them. There's no middle ground.'

'And you?'

'They're okay... in small doses.'

'Can you fluff my pillows up a little, love? I seemed to have slipped down.'

'Of course.'

Eileen leans forward as Zac plumps up the pillows, then takes her gently under the arms and lifts her upright.

'How's that?'

'Much better, thanks. Right, you didn't come here to talk about bagpipes. Katy said you wanted to ask me some questions about my boy, Luke.'

'Yes. That's right.' Before he begins his delicate questioning, Eileen speaks up.

'He was definitely murdered. No two ways about it in my mind.'

'What makes you think that, Eileen?'

'He was terrified of water. I blame myself. When he was about four, I took him to the local pool. I took my eye off him for a split second, and he slipped under. I was busy blowing up the arm bands, and he was sitting on the steps which lead down to the water. Anyway, it was the end of the swimming lessons. I tried again with him on many occasions, but he'd scream blue murder. When Luke's dad died—my first husband, it didn't help.'

'What happened?'

'He used to drink at a couple of pubs next to the canal in the centre of town. One night when he left the pub a thick fog had descended. He somehow ended up in the bottom of a lock. Banged his head on the way down. It traumatised Luke. I took him to a psychologist who diagnosed him with aquaphobia. Luke wasn't a bad lad, you know. He was very loving, and loveable. I know he could be a tyke, always on the cadge, but he had a heart of gold.'

'Why did your daughter not mention this to us?'

'Step-daughter. Not sure. Luke was embarrassed, ashamed about his condition, so we never talked about it.'

'So Katy is not your biological daughter?'

'No. I inherited her when I married my second husband. Worthless bugger. He ran off with his fancy woman when Katy was twelve. Good riddance to bad baggage.'

Zac's mind ponders the new information. Eileen detects the pause.

'Oh, don't get me wrong sergeant, I love Katy like she's my own. You wouldn't find a mother and daughter who were closer. She's been a rock for me over these last two years. Can't be easy. She's young and attractive, and I'm sure she'd rather be out partying and enjoying herself than tending to a dying woman. It's been a tough couple of years for both of us with this damned disease and Luke's addiction.'

She closes her eyes and leans back into her pillow, exhausted by the effort. Her breathing crackles and gurgles.

'Well, lad, are you going to ask me any questions or not?'

'You've sort of answered them all for me already, Eileen. I have one though; why was your solicitor here earlier?'

She laughs, which morphs into a vicious cough. Zac hands her a glass of water.

'Not much of a copper, are you?' she eventually says. 'I updated my will and testament. Katy was insistent. I told her it didn't bloody matter now. I don't have much apart from the house... and the car, not that it's worth much. Everything was due to go to the pair of them. With Luke gone, she'd have got everything, anyway. She said she didn't want any complications, and it was safer to get it down in writing.'

'You mentioned a car?'

'Yes. An old Peugeot. Only worth a couple of grand. Katy can drive, she just hasn't passed her test. Luke never bothered getting lessons.'

'Where do you keep your car?'

'It's at the back of the house. Have you got children, sergeant?'

'Yes, two young boys. Thomas is eight and Samuel is six.'

'Nice names. Never be afraid to show them too much love. You can buy them all the trinkets and baubles in the world, but it's love they need—love and understanding. You must always forgive.'

Zac stands. 'Thanks for your time, Eileen.'

'Going already?' she jokes. He nods. 'Promise me one thing before you go.'

'What?'

'Find whoever did this to my lad. They need to pay for their crime. Justice needs to be done. I'm not sure you'll find the culprit before I'm gone, but your promise is good enough for me.'

Zac takes her hand. 'I promise Eileen. We'll find Luke's killer.'

As he walks back to the car, he tries hard to swallow and remove the aching lump from his throat. He sniffs and dabs at his cheek. Frank was right. Luke wasn't simply a statistic, a thief, a rogue—he was flesh and blood with a beating heart. And at least one person in the world loved him.

15

As Frank makes his way to have another friendly chat with the loan shark, Gareth Brady, he receives Zac's phone call. With the information gleaned from Eileen, it galvanises him to change direction.

Parking in the top car park, he alights from the car, saunters past the tearooms and picks up the trail towards Strid Wood, its dense canopy soon blotting out the daylight. The high-pitched staccato call of a wood warbler interspersed with a descending whistle reverberates through the trees. Things are now clearer in Frank's mind, like the removal of a blockage. The three probable causes of Luke's demise had now become one—he was murdered!

Why would anyone with a morbid fear of water go anywhere near a river—during, or after, a violent thunderstorm?

Frank was on his way to the site where Luke drew his last breath before a torrent of water violently expelled it from his lungs.

Green moss and lichen line the rocks like a badly worn carpet. Frank stares into the abyss of the Strid. Relatively calm today, he imagines what it would have been like on Sunday night after the freak thunderstorm and the floodwater rushed down the river. He'd heard from locals a flash flood could make the water level rise over five feet in a single minute.

Was it Yorkshire hyperbole or the truth?

As he peered into the rushing gorge, here at this bottleneck in the river, he tended to think it was true.

He had to experience what was going through Luke's mind on Sunday night as he teetered on the edge of the rocks, naked, probably shivering, undoubtably terrified.

Did he undergo a rush of aquaphobia?

What was the killer experiencing—fear, excitement, trepidation?

He trawled through his list of suspects, evaluating their personalities, their motives.

Which one of them could push a young man into a hissing cauldron of death?

He realised this was the spot where Luke entered the water. By good fortune, he was found, less than fifty metres downstream where the river once again widens, trapped by a branch. If it hadn't been for the submerged obstacle, Luke's body could have been dragged five, ten, twenty miles away.

The same thought would have passed through the killer's mind. Or maybe—killers?

Luke was tall and fit. Even though he was no fighter, fear should have at least mobilised him in a defence of his life. Or did his phobia, his morbid fear of water, freeze him rigid, and make him mute, weak, vulnerable.

There was only one way the killer brought him here—through Strid Wood via the top car park. It was the shortest and safest route without being seen.

What was the lure, the bait? Money, sex, or was the barrel of a gun or the blade of a knife the only coercion required?

Frank mourns the loss of a young life, a life that had taken the wrong path at some point. Luke was no angel, it was obvious, and although his addiction to gambling provided some mitigating circumstances for his behaviour, it didn't completely exonerate him either. He was healthy, intelligent, and had a caring, loving mother, which was a lot more than some people had. Still, he'd never physically harmed anyone and didn't deserve to die for the errors of his ways.

As Frank walks to the car, he checks the weather forecast on his mobile.

'Damn and blast!'

The intermittent drizzle, which has followed him around for the last few days like a damp shroud, is about to take a turn for the worse with another deluge expected overnight. He taps at the image of Zac and waits.

'Frank?'

'Zac, the weather's about to turn to shit from tonight, so we're racing against the clock. Another deluge will wipe out any remaining evidence. I think it's about time we tried to flush the killer, or killers, out. Now listen carefully.'

Gareth Brady huffs and wheezes his way down the concrete steps, as experienced smokers do. As he exits the piss-stained entrance he bumps into Frank Finnegan.

'Oh, you again. What do you want now? You'll have to walk and talk. I have a client to meet,' he says with a gruff growl.

'A client? You mean a poor, hopeless fool who is so desperate for money they'll agree to your exorbitant interest rates?' Frank replies as he follows in Gareth's footsteps.

Gareth coughs violently. 'We've all got to earn a quid, inspector,' he replies as they set off down a narrow laneway that leads to the back of his premises.

'Do you sleep easy on a night, Gareth?'

'Like a log. If it weren't me, it would be someone else.'

'I suppose that's what drug dealers, sex traffickers, and rapists tell themselves.'

Gareth stops abruptly and swivels to face his antagonist. He pulls out a smoke, sparks, and sucks.

'Don't you dare associate me with that scum!' he bristles. 'I've told you, everything I do is within the law,' he says, raising his voice, clearly agitated by Frank's prodding.

'There is another law—the moral one. Would you offer a loan to your mother at your rates?'

Gareth turns and stomps off. 'The world is a harsh place, inspector. It's dog eat dog.'

'Or kill or be killed?'

'If you've got a question, then ask it. If not, sod off.'

'Where were you last Sunday evening until the early hours of Monday morning?'

'I always spend Sunday with my son. I dropped him back home with his mother about eight. Afterwards, I bought myself a takeaway curry, grabbed a few beers from the supermarket and headed home where I spent the rest of the night.'

Frank is puzzled. Gareth would be of a similar age to himself—mid-fifties. Yet, he talked of his son as though he were a child.

'How old's your son?'

'Twenty-eight. I know what's going through your mind, inspector. My lad has Down syndrome.'

'Oh, I'm sorry.'

'For what? It's not a fucking disease! It's a genetic disorder in a chromosome. I make sure my lad lives life to the full. He brings me great joy.'

'As I'm sure Luke brought great joy to his mum—Eileen.'

Gareth ignores the barb. 'I wish you luck in finding his killer, chief inspector.'

'The noose is tightening. We'll be conducting another extensive search at first light tomorrow using experts and tracker dogs.'

'I heard you'd done that already.'

'We were searching the wrong area. There's another place of interest we need to investigate. I believe it's where Luke's killer either met him or took him.'

Gareth pulls at the door of his immaculately maintained vintage Jaguar. 'Are we done?'

'For now.'

Frank gazes as he drives away. His tactic of getting under Gareth Brady's skin to provoke an outburst hadn't worked. Gareth was a streetwise warrior, too savvy to fall into the trap. But he had proved one thing to Frank—he was human... with feelings.

16

The mechanic is impassive as Zac walks through the gate. He pulls out a rag from his back pocket and wipes his hands.

'What now?' he grizzles.

'And a hello to you too, Dane. A simple question—did you kill Luke Bretton?'

Dane's eyes widen, confused, shocked, scared. 'Are you fucking joking or what?'

'That's not an answer.'

'No! I didn't kill Luke. If I was going to kill him, I'd have done it last year when I caught him fucking up my life! He's still fucking it up now, even when he's dead.'

'Odd—you're not the first person to say that today. Last question—where were you between last Sunday afternoon and early Monday morning?'

'Last Sunday I went around to my mam and dad's for Sunday dinner. Then I watched the match on TV with my old man.'

'Who was playing?'

'Liverpool, Man City.'

'Who won?'

'It was a draw.'

'That game finished about nine-twenty. I watched it myself. What about the rest of the night?'

'I went home. Spent an hour on my desktop then hit the sack. In case you haven't noticed, *officer*, I have a job. I start at eight. Need to be up by six-thirty at the latest. Does that answer your questions?'

Zac ignores him. 'So if I checked with your parents, they'd confirm your alibi?'

'Oh, alibi now, is it—I really am a suspect!'

Zac weathers another aggressive barrage without flinching. 'Dane, you admitted to belting the shit out of Luke last year. You admitted he fucked up your life. Grow up—of course you're a suspect.'

'Yeah, go on then, ask my parents... they'll vouch for me.'

'Of course they will. What parents wouldn't? Jot their address and phone numbers on the back of this, please,' he says, handing him his card and a pen. 'We're near to a breakthrough.'

'Really,' Dane mutters with little interest as he scribbles on the card.

'Yeah. We were looking in the wrong place. We've found the spot where Luke's murderer met him on Sunday night.

Sniffer dogs will be here tomorrow morning. Those things are unreal. They're bound to find something.'

Dane hands the card back. 'Good. Then maybe you'll leave me alone.'

'And how are you feeling today about Luke's death? Sorrow, elation, or is it still ambivalence?'

He glares at Zac. 'Do you really want to know how I feel? I'll tell you. I wish I'd never known Luke Bretton—I wish he'd never been born.'

17

The door is swung open. Loretta Shackleton's blank expression breaks out into a very brief smile.

'Inspector Finnegan, back again so soon. Please come in. My husband is in his study where he seems to spend most of his time these days.'

'I assume he's got a lot of things to work on,' Frank replies.

She closes the door and stares at him. 'May I remind you, inspector, etiquette requires the presumption of good until the opposite is proved,' she states coldly.

'I see you're a follower of Emily Post, the godmother of good manners'.

'You're well read, inspector.'

'It helps with my work. However, I take a more divergent view on things.'

'And your opposing view is?'

'Everyone is a suspect until proved otherwise.'

'Ah, I see. The old Sherlock Holmes mantra—when you eliminate the impossible, whatever remains, however ludicrous, must be the truth?'

'Something like that.'

'Am I a suspect, inspector?'

Frank chuckles. 'Like I said, everyone is a suspect. But not all suspects are created equal.'

'I see.' She turns on her heels and clicks down the hallway. 'Follow me.'

Elliot Shackleton scratches his head, bemused, then hands Frank his mobile phone back.

'Well, yes, it's clear from the photograph, but I'm at a loss inspector. I can honestly say with hand on heart I never noticed the missing pages from the diary when I checked. I must admit, it was a cursory glance. But... it is a puzzle. It was over three months ago, and I had a different secretary at the time, Mrs Fowler. Possibly she spilled something on the pages and once the dates had elapsed, ripped them out... for whatever reason. Unfortunately, it will have to remain a mystery, as she's no longer with us.'

'She's not?' Frank asks.

'Terrible business. She was on her way to pick her dog up from the groomers and a log truck cleaned her up.

He was charged with causing death by dangerous driving. Nevertheless, speed limits for heavy-goods-vehicles will be something I intend to address if the good people of this area elect me as their parliamentary representative at the next election.'

'That is unfortunate.'

Elliot walks around his desk and takes a seat.

'Inspector, you seem to be like a dog with a bone about this business card. I'm not sure how the young man came about it, but I cannot see any connection between the card and his death. I wish I could be of more help.'

'It's a loose end, that's all, and I don't like loose ends. I would be derelict in my duty if I didn't follow up every lead, especially in a murder case.'

A flicker of surprise wings its way across Elliot's face. 'Murder? So you've ruled out suicide and death by misadventure?'

'Yes. One last question, then I'll leave you in peace. Can you tell me where you were between Sunday afternoon and early Monday morning?'

'He was at home, here with me,' Loretta says as she enters the study.

'Yes, that's right,' Elliot confirms.

'All night?'

Loretta slightly adjusts the framed photograph of her husband on the desk.

'Yes. We had Lord and Lady Bybrooke over for afternoon tea. They left about six. Then I prepared our evening meal while Elliot worked on some papers. About seven, we retired to the cinema room and watched a film. Afterwards we ate our dinner, roast beef with spring greens, in the dining room and shortly after we retired to bed, where we both read for a while. We're both early risers and awoke about five-thirty on Monday morning. Would you like me to continue, inspector?'

'No. Your explanation is more than thorough.' Frank turns to leave as Elliot rises to his feet.

'Well, I hope you make a breakthrough in the case. No one wants a killer on the loose. Have you anything major to go on, inspector?'

'We're hoping for a break in the case tomorrow. We've identified where the killer was likely hiding. Tomorrow at first light, we'll be conducting an intensive sweep of the area with a specialist search team. They'll unearth some fresh evidence, I'm sure.'

Elliot and Loretta escort Frank to the door. 'And can we expect another visit from you?' Loretta asks.

Frank smiles. 'No, I think I've exhausted this particular line of enquiry. Please don't take it personally. My sergeant and I have been a nuisance to quite a few people over the last couple of days. It's simply police work.'

'Of course it is,' Elliot says with a beam as he opens the door.

'Good day,' Frank says as he ambles down the stone steps.

18

The bell tinkles as this time Zac performs the duties of flipping the closed sign and dropping the latch on the door. Miles Brandon peers over his spectacles at him with a mixture of trepidation and weariness.

'And how can I help you today, sergeant?'

'Just a few questions. It won't take long.'

Miles pre-empts him. 'Ah, the alibi. I'm afraid it's quite weak and doesn't paint me in a very good light. Early Sunday morning, I actually visited Bolton Abbey.'

'Alone?'

'Yes. I'm a keen birdwatcher. It's a passion of mine. The woods and trails around the river are awash with birdlife and there are numerous hides to make things a little more comfortable.'

'And what time did you leave?'

'I was home by noon and spent the rest of the day and night with my wife.'

'And you didn't leave the house at any time?'

'No. I was back here at the shop on Monday morning before nine.'

'I'll need to speak with your wife to verify your alibi.'

'Fine. I'll give you her number.'

Zac gazes into his eyes, searching for a lie. 'Bit of a coincidence, you visiting the scene where Luke was murdered?'

'I know it doesn't look good, sergeant. But you must realise it's how I spend most Sunday mornings.'

'We'll be searching the place again tomorrow. A different spot this time. We think we've found the area where Luke met with his killer.'

'That's good news, I suppose.'

Zac unlocks the door. 'Oh, one last thing, Mr Brandon. How did Luke first get the job in your shop?'

'He had previous experience working in antiques from his time in London.'

'So, he walked in one day and asked for a job?'

'No. I met him during the run up to the last council elections.'

'Oh?'

'I was a volunteer helping Elliot Shackleton's re-election campaign. He does a lot of excellent work for small businesses.'

Zac's senses tingle. 'Go on?'

19

The two detectives button up their coats against the cold as they retrace the trail Frank took earlier in the day, this time escorted by an estate worker. They walk on in silence as the drizzle turns to gentle rain.

'Bloody weather forecasters have got it wrong again,' Zac grumbles. 'It's not due until later tonight.'

'People have a tendency to remember when people are wrong, but not so much when they're right,' Frank replies.

They amble down the track, the burbling river now distinct. The estate worker stops for a moment and gazes to his left.

'Ah, there it is,' he mutters.

Frank and Zac stare into the labyrinth of trees and shrubs but don't see it. They exchange glances and shrug. They follow the worker along a narrow track, stepping over fallen tree limbs, rubbing up against wet bracken.

'And here we have it,' the worker says, patting the side of the hide built from slats of well-weathered wood.

'Hell, you wouldn't know it was here unless you knew it was here,' Frank says.

'That's why it's called a hide, Frank,' Zac replies.

'Smartarse. Okay, thanks for your assistance. We can find our own way back,' he says to the worker, who is more than happy to abandon them and head back to his own compound out of the rain.

Frank and Zac step inside the structure, which is about six feet by four with an open slot five feet from the forest floor from which to observe the wildlife. A wooden bench is affixed to the back wall.

'It's certainly a damn sight warmer in here,' Zac remarks.

'Aye, it's not a bad little bolt hole,' he says thoughtfully as he sizes up the inside. 'Perfect place for a bit of illicit sex.'

'Frank, I like you a lot, but I'm not that way inclined.'

Frank grins at him. 'Daft bugger,' he replies. 'Right, don your rubber gloves and turn your torch on. You investigate the outside. I'll take the inside.'

'Funny about that,' Zac says, stepping back into the rain.

Frank pulls on his gloves as his torch beam begins a slow scan of the interior.

'What exactly are we looking for?' Zac calls out.

'Are you sure you're a detective sergeant... sergeant?'

'Pretty sure.'

'Well, then—engage your detective brain.'

'Only asking,' Zac's disembodied voice mumbles.

'With the latest information we've gathered today, I think we've narrowed our suspects down to two... possibly three.'

'Apart from Katy Kennedy's alibi, all the others were next to useless. Relatives or partners vouched for them, which in my book means nothing,' Zac calls out.

'Don't rule out Katy based on her version of events.'

'I saw her Uber receipt corresponding with the times she gave me. And she doesn't have a car registered to her—I checked. But her mother has a car.'

'What if once she got back home, she took the car and met Luke for whatever reason? The Uber receipt merely a ruse. It's the smart ones who produce believable alibis.'

'Possible, I suppose. Until we get access to their phone records, we won't know.'

They continue their elusive search to no avail for another five minutes.

'I think we're clutching at straws, Frank,' Zac says as he enters the hide, shaking the water from his coat.

'Hmm... you might be right. It was worth a shot.'

'Are we still continuing with the stakeout tonight? Even if the suspect does turn up, we can't charge them with anything. I know it means they're guilty, but we need evidence.'

'At least it will help us focus our resources and attention on one suspect. So yes, the stakeout is going ahead.' He checks his watch. 'It's gone five. Come on, let's head back to the pub, get a warm shower then a quick bite to eat.'

'What time are we coming back?'

'The car park officially shuts at seven, so we'll return just after. I can't see our killer surfacing until after eight at the earliest.'

'If at all.'

Frank shines his torch into Zac's face, making him scrunch his eyes up. 'There's a negative side to you that needs to be kept in check, sergeant.'

They amble out into the rainfall as Frank spins around and peers one last time into the hide. The smallest of reflections catches his attention.

'Eh up, what have we here?'

Zac follows his gaze. 'Could be the eye of a shrew or mouse,' Zac offers.

'Doubt it. I've been clomping around in there like a Clydesdale in labour. Shine your torch in the corner and don't lose sight of it.'

'Boss.'

Frank creeps back in but loses contact with the shiny object.

'Damn it, I've lost it.'

'You're blocking my beam. Get on your knees and edge forward,' Zac advises.

A cacophony of moans and groans rings out as Frank awkwardly lowers himself to his knees and crawls towards the corner of the hut.

'I'm getting too old for this bloody game,' he grizzles. 'Meera was right, I should have taken early retirement a couple of years back.'

'It's never too late.'

'What are you trying to say?'

'Nothing.'

'I've lost it again.'

'About another foot to your right. That's it, a bit more… stop. It's directly below the bench seat. You're right on top of it.'

Frank's eyes slowly adjust until they latch onto the object. He reaches out and delicately pinches it between thumb and forefinger. He pulls himself up, cracking the back of his head on the bench seat.

'Holy shit on a stick,' he cries, vigorously rubbing the back of his skull with his free hand.

'What is it?'

'I banged my bloody head.'

'I'm not bothered about that. What did you find?'

He holds the object out in front of Zac. 'I think we've found our killer.'

20

Thunder rumbles down the U-shaped valleys of Wharfedale, billowing out over saturated fields, echoing through stone built hamlets, reverberating in woods and spinneys. Distant sheet lightning occasionally blisters the sky as weak moonlight flickers through low-hanging mist, creating a milky ethereal hue. The countryside is a gothic backdrop to a stage play yet to begin. The actors wait in the wings with nervous anticipation for the opening curtain.

Two plain clothed officers are each respectively sitting in the estate's two tearooms—one near the river, the other next to the car park on top of Strid Wood. A pair of unmarked police cars are concealed in fields behind drystone walls—one to the south and one to the north of the upper car park. And two senior detectives are shivering in a draughty hide that drips rainwater onto them in the middle of a wood.

'Christ, you wouldn't send a dog out in this weather, and that storm is heading our way. I think my balls have turned to ice,' Zac laments, looking at his watch. 'Nine-thirty. How much longer?'

Frank sighs. 'As long as it takes.'

'Hell. I'm not going to get my pint of Guinness tonight,' he replies forlornly.

Frank smiles, although he cannot be seen. 'That's where you're wrong, Zac.'

'What do you mean?'

Frank taps his head. 'Upstairs for thinking, downstairs for dancing. I had a word with the landlord after our rushed meal. Without mentioning specifics, I told him we could be in for a long and chilly night. Seems he's an enthusiastic fan of the police. In fact, he thinks we're wonderful. He gave me a key to the main bar. Said if we arrived back after he and his missus had locked up and gone to bed, then to let ourselves into the bar and help ourselves to a few pints—on the house. He even said he'd throw a few logs on the fire for us, make sure it was still nice and cosy.'

'Brilliant!' Zac exclaims, rubbing his hands together.

'I'm not such an ogre after all. I understand life and it's the simple things which oil the wheels.'

Silence ensues as the rain intensifies, the river rises, and the mournful hoot of an owl echoes spookily across the wood.

'I was thinking, Frank.'

'First time for everything. What about?'

'It could have been a plant by the real killer.'

'I've thought of that. That's why we already have search warrants and forensics on standby. We'll need to move quickly. If I've got this wrong, we're going to cop a good hiding—at least I am. You were following instructions from a senior officer—got it?'

'Yes, boss.'

'The first time we questioned Katy Kennedy, did you notice her fingers?'

'Erm... not particularly.'

'Her left hand, ring finger.'

'What about it?'

'There was a white band where a ring used to sit. Which means?'

'She could have been in a relationship which recently ended?'

'Yes. Or?'

'She lost it in some sort of struggle?'

'Yes. Or?'

'It was on the windowsill, above the sink. She'd taken it off to wash the pans and forgot to put it back on.'

'Well done. Everything our senses detect may have a plausible or implausible explanation. Always keep an open mind until the facts are overwhelming or irrefutable. But never let who you want to be the killer override the evidence.

I've seen it a lot in my time and a good defence counsel will eat the case alive.'

Zac lifts himself from the bench seat and blows on his hands. 'I had a nightmare last night,' he states as he bends to peer out through the slot in the hide, seeing nothing.

'What about?'

'I was with Tom and Sam, crossing the river on steppingstones. Kelly was on the bank, urging us to come back, all worried and agitated. Sam was on my shoulders, Thomas ahead. The river was shallow, calm. There was a distant rumble—not thunder—something else. I looked upstream and saw this wave heading our way. Not huge, like a sea wave, but about three or four foot in height. I shouted at Tom to turn around. We skipped along the stones and Kelly grabbed Sam from my shoulders. I turned around and Tom was frozen in fear as he gazed at the rushing wave. I leapt back across the stones, but before I could reach him, it hit us. We both fell into the water. I surfaced and tried to grab him, but I couldn't reach. The current was too powerful. Kept pulling us both under. He drifted to the left, then the right, like a barrel. Eventually I clutched his arm and pulled him in close to me with the cries of Kelly and Sam ringing out, way behind us. For a moment, I felt safe. I'd rescued my lad. The current momentarily eased before the undertow grabbed me. It was powerful, like a suction that I was too weak to fight. We both went under and when I resurfaced, I saw it…' He tails off and pauses, reflects.

'Saw what?'

'The boulders of the Strid, rushing towards us. It was horrifying. My heart was pounding, I couldn't swallow, I had no breath, my strength was gone.'

'And?' Frank prompts.

'Don't know. I woke up in a cold sweat.'

'Hmm… remind me to never share a room with you.'

The police radio attached to Zac's lapel crackles into life.

"Suspect's vehicle has passed the upper car park. Is now slowly doing a three-point turn," the officer in the tearoom begins.

'Can you tell how many people are in the vehicle?' Zac asks.

"Hard to tell. Definitely one, at least."

Zac mutes the radio. 'You don't fucking say,' he mumbles to Frank. 'What's our recruitment process these days?'

"Suspect has now parked up twenty metres from the car park, alighted from the vehicle and is travelling on foot towards the nature trail."

Zac mutes the radio again. 'Travelling on foot? What else were they expected to travel by? Camel, elephant, helicopter, skateboard? Give me strength!' He unmutes the radio. 'Received and understood. Everyone to maintain radio silence until further notice. Out.'

Frank twitches, coming alive. 'Switch it off altogether. We don't want one of them accidentally transmitting and scaring the suspect off.'

Zac flicks the switch.

'Take up your designated position outside, Zac. I don't think for one moment they'll do a runner. But who really knows the mind of a killer?'

He departs to the sound of cracking branches and the scrunch of vegetation underfoot.

A few minutes elapse until a dancing beam of torchlight materialises through the gloomy wood. It flickers up and down, left and right, seemingly uncoordinated. Frank steadies himself to the right of the entrance. Tentative footsteps edge onward in the direction of the hide. More illumination, searching, suspicious.

Breathing. Barely discernible above the pitter-patter of raindrops, the gushing river, the noise of nocturnal animal life.

Frank braces as the floor of the hide is lit up in a pure white light.

A body walks in, swaying the torch from side to side.

'Good of you to join us,' Frank remarks as a startled scream pierces the cocoon of the cloying night.

21

She calms, realising he's no physical threat. Zac walks up behind her, blocking any escape.

'Is this what you were looking for?' he says as he holds the Mikimoto cultured pearl earring in front of her, illuminated by his torch.

'Yes, inspector. That's exactly what I was looking for.'

'Obviously lost it here?'

'My husband is a keen ornithologist.'

'You don't say. They're ten-a-penny around these parts.'

'We often frequent the hides in this wood. It's not my idea of fun, but one must cater to one's partner's tastes occasionally to sustain a happy relationship.'

'And when were you and your husband here last?'

'Two, three weeks ago. I remember walking through a spider's web. It startled me and I rubbed around my head and face. I must have shed the earring then. It is quite valuable, inspector. Not that I'd expect you to know. When you said you were about to instigate a new search tomorrow,

I wondered if it would include this hide. I was worried one of your officers may find it and pocket it for themselves.'

'Wow! You're good!' Frank says as he nods at Zac, the predetermined signal to unleash forensics at Uplands Manor. 'The earring—it may be valuable to a man on my wages. But to you, it's pin-money. I bought the exact same pair for my wife the other day, from a shop you frequent regularly, run by Miles Brandon. Of course, you know Miles well, don't you, Mrs Shackleton? You are one of his best patrons. And he's also a big supporter of your husband's political career. Even volunteered at the last local elections. And that's where he met Luke Bretton. I believe you were the campaign manager? Funny how your husband didn't recognise a young, attractive lad who was part of his re-election campaign when I showed him Luke's photo.'

'We don't get to know all the volunteers.'

'Tell it to the jury. Loretta Shackleton, I am arresting you on suspicion of the murder of Luke Bretton. You do not have to say anything, but it may harm your defence if you do not mention when questioned something which you later rely on in court. Anything you do say may be given in evidence.'

'You'll regret this, Chief Inspector Finnegan. You're making a big mistake. My husband has many influential and powerful friends.'

'Arms behind your back. I'm about to cuff you.'

'My God! Is this really necessary?'

'No. But I need to get some pleasure out of the job.'

22

Thursday 10th April 11:55 pm

The fire is weak. Frank picks up the poker and stabs at the embers, then throws a couple of logs on top. Within seconds, they erupt into a crimson dance, radiating heat.

'Who's doing the honours?' Zac asks.

'You can.'

'What's your poison?' he says, making his way behind the bar.

'Timothy Taylor's dark ale.'

'Pint?'

'Don't ask stupid questions.'

'Coming right up, Frank.'

'Oh, and a couple of packets of pork scratchings. I'm feeling peckish.'

Both men pull their chairs close to the fire. Although physically exhausted their minds are still racing.

'So how do you think it will play out tomorrow, Frank?'

'Her barrister is flying up from London first thing in the morning. Bernard Ogilvy, one of the best defence lawyers in the land. The interview is scheduled for nine o'clock. He'll advise her to say nothing, so we'll play a game of—no comment for twenty minutes, then haul her off to the courts to charge her. She'll probably get bail.'

'What! On a murder charge?'

'They'll no doubt bring in some witnesses to vouch for her outstanding character, set bail at a couple of million, and she'll be free to go. To be fair, she's hardly the type to do a runner.'

'I bet if Katy Kennedy had been the killer, they wouldn't let her out on bail.'

Frank puts his pint down, appearing shocked. 'Are you suggesting this great nation of ours is still based on an ancient feudal system where the wealthy, and powerful receive preferential treatment on the sweet, merciful sword of justice?'

'Aye. Too bloody right I am.'

'That's the problem with you Scots—you're still fighting battles you lost two hundred years ago.'

'Codswallop. Anyway, why do you think Loretta murdered Luke?'

'Extortion and her husband's future political career. I think she first met Luke when he volunteered to help Elliot Shackleton's re-election campaign. Then Loretta would have seen a bit of him in the antique shop, as she's a regular patron. I guess they struck up a friendship, which then became a sexual relationship. He probably tapped her up for handouts, fifty, a hundred quid here and there. When Elliot was earmarked as the next candidate for parliament, she probably ended the relationship with Luke. Too risky, she couldn't afford any scandal to jeopardise his career trajectory. That's when I think Luke probably began to blackmail her.'

'Do you think Elliot was aware of all this?'

'Not sure... probably. If not at the beginning, then certainly by the end, when the extortion started. I think that's what the business card points to. Maybe Loretta was playing hardball, so Luke met with Elliot and asked for money—or else.'

'He'd go to the papers?'

'Yes,' Frank says taking a hefty gulp of the creamy dark liquid.

'None of it is provable in court unless she confesses.'

'That's right. Mere supposition and conjecture. I can hear Bernard Ogilvy now parading up and down in front of the jury, laughing at the very idea. That's why the forensics was critical. Finding burnt remnants of Luke's clothing is irrefutable evidence. They can't argue that one away.'

'What first alerted you to the theory?'

'When I called at Uplands Manor, I noticed a smouldering pile of grass clippings. I asked Loretta about the gardens and if she was the one who maintained them. She laughed and said no. They employ a full-time gardener, but she said he was on holiday. I didn't give it a second thought at the time. But my mind kept coming back to Luke's clothes. Where the hell were they? The divers combed the river twice, from Burnsall down to Addingham. If Luke's clothes had been swept into the water by the flood, then something should have turned up. Especially a hoody. That would have got snagged on something. I knew then the killer had taken Luke's clothes. And what's more incriminating than being caught with the victim's clothes? She had to get rid of them and what better way than burning them? It was her first mistake. If she'd dropped the clothes into the water, we'd have assumed misadventure.'

'And her second mistake was losing the earring in the hide. Do you think she had sex with him in there?'

'Probably. A farewell present, before she handed over the money he'd demanded—not that she was ever going to do that.'

'But how did she lure him down to the Strid?'

'Hmm... not sure. He certainly wouldn't have ventured anywhere near a swollen river on his own volition. I can only assume she had a gun or a knife,' Frank says as he gazes into the playful flames, face hardened. 'His last few moments on earth would have been absolutely terrifying. Killed by the very thing he'd feared all his life—aquaphobia. It makes my blood run cold to think of it. Anyway, our part of the process is nearly over. We'll gather all our evidence together, finalise our reports and hand it over to the CPS.'

'I'm looking forward to going home tomorrow. This business has left a nasty taste in my mouth.'

'You're not wrong. Let Luke's demise be a salutary lesson for you Zac.'

'And what does that mean?'

'Gambling.'

'Ah! Away with you, man. I have a wee flutter on the horses now and again and the occasional fiver in a slot machine. It's hardly comparable to Luke's compulsive addiction.'

'Addictions are like a tumour, Zac. They start small and, if left unchecked, they grow. Just saying.'

'Thanks for the advice.'

'In the morning, I want you to visit Eileen at the hospice, and tell her we've charged Loretta Shackleton with her son's murder. It may bring her some comfort. At least she won't be around for the trial, which will be a media circus. A high-society woman fraternising with a young, handsome, unemployed lad. Sex, extortion, and murder—can you imagine the salacious headlines? They'll have a bloody field day. I suppose it's a blessing in disguise Eileen won't witness it.'

'I think it will be the end of Elliot Shackleton's glittering political career even before it got started.'

'Oh, yes. They'll drop him like a ton of bricks. Unless she gets off and there's not much chance of that. Right, one for the road, then it's time to hit the sack. My shout!' he says as he swallows the last of his pint in three thirsty gulps.

'Your generosity knows no bounds, Frank, considering it's on the house.'

23

Ten Months Later – Final Day of the Crown Versus Loretta Shackleton

Frank and Zac scamper up the steps of the courthouse, an imposing eighteenth century stone structure in classic Georgian style, impressive, elegant, imposing.

'I'm feeling nervous,' Zac says as they enter the reception.

'How many times have you given evidence in court?' Frank says with incredulity.

'Yes, I know. But this is such a high-profile case, and I'm wondering why the defence is calling me so late in proceedings. They questioned you two days ago.'

Frank halts and turns to his young officer. 'They'll probably try to trip you up on something, which means they're desperate. But there's nothing to be nervous about. Take the stand and answer the questions to the best of your ability,' Frank replies as he pulls out a packet of Polo mints. 'Bernard Ogilvy is a canny operator. Don't argue the point with him. Don't be snarky or come across as cocky. You're a professional police officer and most of the jury will respect the police. They're on your side. Mint?'

'No, thanks. Do you think she'll go down?'

'Undoubtably. I'm looking forward to seeing her squirm in the witness stand today. It doesn't matter how often they bang on about her good character, her charity work, her unblemished record, there's one thing she can't wriggle out of—Luke Bretton's burnt clothes under a pile of grass clippings in her garden. Let's hope it's all wrapped up today. Our workload is mounting, and we've got better things to do, like solving the murder of Shirley Fox, and capturing those bastards who are holding-up petrol stations.'

'Aye, you're right. I best go to the witness room. I'll see you later.'

'Good luck.'

Frank is seated in the public gallery. Zac shoots him a glance before he takes to the witness stand and swears the oath. Bernard Ogilvy, barrister for the defence, eyeballs him intently for a moment.

'Sergeant Stoker, how old are you?'

'Thirty two.'

'And how long have you been a police officer?'

'I'm in my tenth year.'

'And how long as a detective?'

'Four years.'

'In those four years has DCI Finnegan always been your superior?'

'Yes.'

'You have a close working relationship?'

'Yes, we do.'

'Do you regard him as a good detective?'

Barrister for the prosecution rises. 'Objection, your honour. Irrelevant. DCI Finnegan is not in the witness stand.'

'I'm merely trying to find out the working relationship between the two leading detectives in this case, Your Honour,' Ogilvy counters.

The judge peers down his nose at him. 'Objection overruled, but don't labour the point, Mr Ogilvy. The witness will answer the question.'

Zac shuffles. 'Yes. DCI Finnegan is one of the best.'

'In what way?'

'He's fair, measured, thorough. He considers things carefully before drawing his conclusions.'

'I see. When you first began investigating the death of Luke Bretton, you weren't sure as to why his body was in the river, were you?'

'No. But it's not unusual at the beginning of an investigation.'

'You weren't sure whether it was homicide, suicide, or death by misadventure?'

'That's correct.'

'But at some stage during the investigation, you, or DCI Finnegan, decided it was a homicide. Can you explain how you reached your conclusion?'

'I paid a visit to Luke's mother, Eileen Bretton, in Burnley Hospice. She was dying of cancer. It was during the visit she informed me Luke suffered from aquaphobia. He'd nearly drowned as a young boy and later on his father died when he fell into a canal lock.'

'Aquaphobia is an extreme psychological fear of water, a clinical medical condition, is it not?'

'I believe so.'

'Was it this information which made you believe Luke was murdered?'

'Yes.'

'And was the decision yours or DCI Finnegan's?'

'We both came to the same conclusion. There's no way anyone with aquaphobia would end up in a swollen river.'

'Because their morbid fear would prevent them from going anywhere near the water?'

'Yes.'

'Do you know if Luke was ever treated for his condition?'

'Erm... I don't know. His mother did say she'd taken him to a psychologist when he was younger. He was the one who diagnosed the condition.'

'Did you check?'

'Sorry?'

'Did you check Luke's medical records?'

'Erm... no.'

'A moment ago you said DCI Finnegan was measured, thorough. That he considers things carefully before drawing his conclusions. But you didn't check Luke Bretton's medical history?'

'Erm, well... in a murder investigation...'

'It's a simple yes or no answer, sergeant?'

'Objection, Your Honour! The witness has already answered the question.'

'Sustained.'

Bernard Ogilvy turns away from Zac and stares at the floor. 'So your belief Luke suffered from aquaphobia was based purely on the word of his mother, Eileen Bretton?'

'Yes. She had no reason to make it up.'

'Indeed, why would she? Defence counsel has done an extensive search of Luke's medical history and nowhere were we able to find the mystery psychologist. Can you explain that, Sergeant Stoker?'

'No, I can't. Even so, I see no reason for Eileen to lie.'

'A dying woman, under heavy medication, losing her only son. If, in fact, Luke had taken his own life, in her mind she would see it as a failure on her own part as a mother, a protector, would she not?'

'I don't see the correlation.'

'Do you have children, sergeant?'

'Objection, Your Honour! Irrelevant.'

'Overruled. The witness will answer the question.'

'Yes, I do. Two young boys.'

'And God forbid, but if something were to happen to one of them, even if it were out of your control, would you feel a sense of guilt?'

'Aye, I suppose I would.'

'Why?'

'Because as a parent, it's our job to make sure no harm comes to them.'

'Exactly. I believe Eileen thought the same.'

'Objection! Supposition, Your Honour. The defence counsel cannot possibly know what Eileen Bretton thought.'

'Withdrawn. I believe Eileen Bretton couldn't accept Luke took his own life, the guilt was too much and therefore concocted this story about aquaphobia and in doing so led you and DCI Finnegan down a blind alley of murder. Is that not the case, sergeant?'

'Not in my opinion.'

'Not in your opinion. Let's move on. At the beginning of the case, you had five suspects you questioned. Is that correct?'

'I wouldn't call them suspects. More like people of interest.'

'Oh, come sergeant, don't play semantics. Suspects, people of interest—they're one and the same, aren't they?'

'Not really.'

'Very well... there were five people of interest you questioned?'

'Yes.'

'Tell me about Dane King.'

'Dane used to be the best friend of Luke. When Luke returned from London, they struck up their friendship again. Dane nipped home one lunchtime and caught Luke and his fiancé having sex.'

'And how did Dane react?'

'He gave Luke a good hiding.'

'He assaulted him?'

'Yes.'

'So, a violent man. Were his actions justifiable in your opinion?'

'Objection, Your Honour.'

'Sustained.'

'I'll rephrase the question. Dane King proved he was capable of violence on his best friend?

'It appears so. Not justifiable but hardly surprising considering the circumstances.'

'And bearing in mind this incident took place about a year before Luke's death, when you questioned Dane about his current feelings towards Luke, what did he say?'

'He said he hated him and wished Luke had never been born.'

'Let's move on to person of interest number two, Katy Kennedy, Luke's stepsister by marriage. What was Katy's reaction to Luke's death?'

'She didn't appear too concerned.'

'How would you describe the relationship between Luke and Katy?'

'It was obvious she didn't like him.'

'Can you elaborate?'

'When Eileen remarried, Luke resented it. Katy was also bitter about Luke's gambling addiction and the way Eileen Bretton had to bail Luke out until she had no savings left, and at a time when she was fighting cancer.'

'So, a lot of bitterness?'

'I'd say so, yes.'

'Did Eileen Bretton own her house?'

'Yes.'

'And after her death, were you aware who the beneficiaries were?'

'Eileen told me it would have been split equally between Katy and Luke.'

'I see. And with Luke's death, it's safe to assume Katy would have inherited the lot.'

'Yes. Eileen changed her will the day I visited her.'

'On her own volition?'

'Ahem, no. Katy organised for a solicitor to visit Eileen at the hospice.'

'Hmm... rather cold and mercenary, wouldn't you say?'

'I'd call it pragmatic.'

Ogilvy lifts his head and gazes into the gallery. 'Tell us about the moneylender, Gareth Brady.'

'Luke owed Mr Brady five thousand pounds and had been avoiding him.'

'How would you describe Mr Brady's business? Is it a modern, state-of-the-art affair with high-street frontage, a place which would engender confidence and trust in customers?'

'Not really. It's old school.'

'In what way?'

'Back alley sort of thing.'

'Would you say it is based on fear?'

'Fear?'

'Yes, fear. Mr Brady used to be a professional boxer many years ago and has a criminal conviction for assault and battery, attributes which would come in handy in ensuring customers repaid their loans. Wouldn't you agree?'

'Possibly.'

'Tell the court about person of interest number four—Miles Brandon, the proprietor of Treasure Chest antique shop.'

'Luke worked for Mr Brandon in the shop for about a year before he left.'

'Left? Did he go voluntarily or was he given the sack?'

'He left voluntarily after Mr Brandon confronted Luke and another member of staff about the cash till being down. He did a stocktake and noticed a few items were missing, most notably an antique wristwatch.'

'And what was the value of the watch?'

'Twenty-five thousand pounds.'

'That's a lot of money.'

'It is.'

'Did Miles report it to the police?'

'No. He went to see Luke to get the watch back, but he'd sold it online to a private buyer. Miles said he had no alternative but to report it to the police... for the insurance.'

'But he didn't?'

'No. Luke threatened him, not physically.'

'Then how?'

'Ahem... he said he'd tell Mr Brandon's wife about their affair.'

'So Luke and Miles Brandon were in a sexual relationship?'

'I'm not sure it was a relationship. More like casual sex was the impression I formed.'

'And did Miles pay Luke for sex?'

'He said he gave him money after sex, as Luke was always short.'

'Isn't that the same as paying for sex?'

'I suppose.'

'A business transaction?'

'Yes, I guess.'

'We'll move on to our last person of interest—Elliot Shackleton. Why did he interest you?'

'We found Mr Shackleton's council business card in Luke's bedroom, with a day and time scribbled on the back of it.'

'And?'

'That's all.'

'That's all?'

'We follow up all leads in a murder investigation.'

'You didn't follow up on Eileen Bretton's mystery psychologist, did you, sergeant?'

'No.'

'So, five suspects altogether?'

'Persons of interest, yes.'

'I beg your pardon, sergeant—persons of interest. Would you care to turn around and identify the accused in the dock?'

'I don't have to turn around. I know who it is.'

'Please sergeant, humour an old man.'

Zac slowly spins around and gazes through the glass windows of the dock. Loretta Shackleton stares back, demure, composed, impassive.

'Tell me who you see?' Ogilvy quizzes. 'Is the accused Katy Kennedy, Dane King, Miles Brandon, Gareth Brady, or Elliot Shackleton?'

'No. The accused is Loretta Shackleton.'

'That's right, the accused is Loretta Shackleton,' Ogilvy adds with a wistful sigh before launching into a vociferous tirade. 'Not once in your investigation did you question her, did you sergeant?' he yells.

'No.'

'Not once was she a person of interest?'

'Not in the early...'

'Not once did you show her the photo of Luke Bretton?'

'No, but...'

'Not once did you ask her if she knew Luke Bretton?'

'Well... no, it was only after...'

'Thorough, measured, considered? I'd say it's sloppy police work, guessing games, and incompetence!' he ends with a flourish of the arms as murmuring swells in the public gallery.

'Objection, Your Honour. Harassing the witness!'

'Sustained.'

'I have no further questions, Your Honour.'

'The witness may stand down. Court will retire for a fifteen minute recess,' the judge declares.

Frank places the tray on the table and takes a seat opposite Zac.

'Christ, he was brutal,' Zac murmurs, still slightly dazed by the withering verbal bombardment he'd endured.

'Ogilvy's good, I'll give him that. It's nothing personal, Zac. It's his job to muddy the waters and distract the jury from the irrefutable evidence. But Loretta's up next, and it's our turn to unleash hell. Just keep reminding yourself about the clothes in her garden. It's the smoking gun. Everything else is simply fluff,' he says as he dispenses the coffee.

24

With Loretta Shackleton standing in the witness box, and oath sworn, the barrister for the prosecution begins.

'Mrs Shackleton, how old are you?'

'Thirty-five.'

'And your husband?'

'Forty-eight.'

'Bit of an age gap?'

'Not really. Thirteen years isn't the great chasm it used to be.'

'No, possibly not. How long have you been married?'

'We celebrated our tenth wedding anniversary earlier this year.'

'Is it a happy marriage?'

'Blissfully so.'

'Blissfully so! Surely all marriages have their difficulties?'

'I'm no expert in other people's marriages, but our marriage is stable, loving and built on trust, fidelity, and mutual respect.'

'Did you know Luke Bretton, Mrs Shackleton?'

'Yes, although I didn't know his last name until after I was arrested and charged.'

'So how did you know him?'

'Eighteen-months ago my husband ran for re-election as a local councillor. I organised his campaign. Council elections don't have quite the same glamour as a general election, but still require meticulous organisation, something I'm particularly good at. I recruited a small team comprising Mrs Fowler, who was Elliot's former council secretary, sadly now deceased. And the other two volunteers were Miles Brandon and Luke Bretton, but I only knew him as Luke at that point.'

'Yes, you've already mentioned that. Why did you not know his last name?'

'I never got around to asking him.'

'And what tasks were the volunteers given?'

'Door knocking, leafleting, that sort of thing.'

'Did your husband ever meet Luke Bretton?'

'Not to my knowledge.'

'Wasn't that a bit rude? Here we have a young man giving up his time for free on your husband's behalf and he doesn't have the courtesy to introduce himself?'

'Objection, Your Honour. If my learned friend wishes to ask the question, then it should be addressed to Mr Shackleton.'

'Sustained.'

'Mrs Shackleton were you having, or did you ever have, a sexual relationship with Luke Bretton?'

'No. The very idea is preposterous. As I mentioned, I'm happily married and I take my marriage vows, under the oath of God, very seriously, as does my husband.'

'Did you find Luke Bretton attractive?'

'Objection, Your Honour. The question is irrelevant.'

'Overruled. The defendant shall answer the question.'

'Luke was handsome in his own way, but he was nothing more than a boy.'

'A boy?'

'Yes.'

'He was twenty-five, Mrs Shackleton. He was closer to you in age than your husband. After all, age is not the chasm it used to be.'

'Objection, Your Honour. The prosecution is making a statement, not asking a question.'

'Sustained.'

'Mrs Shackleton, did you take Luke Bretton to the hide in Strid Wood, have sex with him, then lure him to his death by pushing him into the River Wharfe near the Strid?'

'No.'

'Your Honour, I'd like to show the jury exhibit A. It's a pearl earring found in the hide at Strid Wood.'

'Is this your earring, Mrs Shackleton?'

'Yes. My husband bought them for me for our tenth wedding anniversary.'

'Can you tell the jury your movements on the night of April 10, of this year, Mrs Shackleton?'

'Certainly. I had misplaced one of my pearl earrings some weeks before and was at a loss to know where it may be. I then remembered that two weeks before, I had accompanied my husband to Strid Wood early one Sunday morning. He's a keen ornithologist. We spent about an hour in a hide. I took a book to read as I'm not particularly interested in my husband's hobby. As I sat down on a bench, I brushed across a cobweb. I flailed at my head and face to make sure I didn't have a spider on me. I wondered if it was at that moment, I'd lost my precious earring. On the night in question, April 10th, I drove to Strid Wood and made my way to the hide. I'd been correct in my suspicion, but unfortunately, I was arrested by DCI Finnegan, who had indeed found the missing earring.'

'What time of day was it, when you returned to the hide, Mrs Shackleton?'

'Oh, about nine-thirty, give or take.'

'And what was the weather like?'

'Cold, drizzly.'

'Dark?'

'Becoming dark, yes.'

'It wasn't cold and drizzly, Mrs Shackleton. At nine-thirty a full blown thunderstorm was underway. And yet despite the conditions, and being a single female, alone, you ventured out in the dark to search in a desolate wood for your so-called precious earring, which in fact cost two hundred and fifty pounds.'

'An item can be precious in more than a monetary value. The earring held sentimental value.'

'I put it to you, Mrs Shackleton, the real reason you went out in such foreboding conditions was because earlier in the day, DCI Finnegan had paid your husband a second visit. As he was leaving, he said the police were to launch a new search the following morning in Strid Wood. You knew if the police found the earring, it could lead back to you. Isn't this the truth, Mrs Shackleton?'

'No.'

'Your Honour, I'd like the jury to see exhibits, B, C, and D. The exhibits are the burnt remnants of the clothes Luke Bretton was last seen wearing before his death. Do you accept that Mrs Shackleton?'

'Yes. I've no reason to doubt the police forensics. They do an excellent job.'

'Mrs Shackleton, can you explain to the court how Luke's clothes ended up at the bottom of a pile of grass clipping which you set fire to on Tuesday April 8, two days after Luke's death?'

'Yes, I can. My husband and I are early risers and like to start the day off with a brisk forty-minute walk. On that particular Tuesday, we were finishing our usual circuit and on our way back home. As we turned the last corner, I spotted a carrier bag poking out from overgrown grass on the side of the road. I abhor litter. On inspecting the bag, I saw they were clothes, and not in the best of condition. I took them home to dispose of them. If they had been in good condition, I would have washed them and donated them to the charity shop.'

'Mrs Shackleton, may I remind you that you're under oath?'

'I am well aware of that. And if you're inferring I'm lying, you can verify my account with my husband.'

'I'm sure I can. Back to the clothes. Why burn them? Why not simply put them in the dustbin?'

'The grass was getting a little out of control, and with our gardener away on holiday, I mowed the lawns myself. The compost bin was full, so I thought the best way to get rid of the clippings was to have a small garden fire. With all the rain we'd recently had, I knew it would be hard to light. Then I remembered the bag of discarded clothes. I placed them under the clippings, added a little diesel, then lit the fire.'

'And you expect me to believe that?'

'I cannot control what you believe. But it is the truth.'

Bernard Ogilvy surveys the courtroom, his kingdom, his battleground. 'Mrs Shackleton, I believe you and your husband do a lot of work for charity.'

'That's correct, but it's not something we talk about.'

'And why is that?'

'We don't do it for kudos, or to appear virtuous. We do it because we've both been extremely fortunate in life. My husband and I have built up two highly successful businesses over the last decade and we are financially stable and enjoy many of the perks of success. A few years ago, we decided it was time to give something back and help the less fortunate in our society.'

'And what charities do you help?'

'Objection Your Honour, is there any relevance to the questions?'

'Sustained. Mr Ogilvy, I think you've ascertained Mrs Shackleton and her husband are generous benefactors. Now move your line of questioning along.'

'Yes, Your Honour. DCI Finnegan paid two visits to your home after the discovery of Luke Bretton's body?'

'That's correct.'

'Did he at any point show you a photo of Luke?'

'No.'

'Did he ask you if you knew Luke Bretton?'

'No.'

'Did your husband ever mention the name—Luke Bretton to you after the first police visit?'

'No. He said the police were investigating the death of a young man found in the River Wharfe. Elliot said one of his business cards had been found in the man's bedroom. And that was the end of our conversation regarding the matter.'

'Mrs Shackleton did you murder Luke Bretton?'

'No, I did not.'

'No further questions, Your Honour.'

The barrister for the prosecutions stalks up and down in front of the jurors, creating tension and drama.

'There are a lot of red herrings and detritus in court cases, none more so than in a murder trial. However, you must focus your minds and separate the wheat from the chaff and look at the facts and also… improbabilities. Let's refresh ourselves of the facts.

Mrs Shackleton, four days after the death of Luke Bretton, returns to the hide where she says she lost her earring. At nine-thirty at night, during a treacherous thunderstorm, she trails out, alone, to search for her missing earring—an earring worth two hundred and fifty pounds for the pair.

Really? In the middle of a wood, a young attractive woman, scratching around for her not so precious earring? Is it plausible? No, it is not. The reason Loretta Shackleton returned to the hide that night was to locate an earring which would implicate her in the murder of Luke Bretton. There is no other plausible explanation.

Then there are Luke's clothes. How convenient Luke's would-be killer should gather up his clothes, put them in a plastic carrier bag and deposit them on a grass verge not more than two hundred metres from the Shackleton's home. That is one hell of a coincidence. Forensics proved they are the clothes Luke was last seen in, as described by his stepsister, Katy Kennedy. They just happen to end up at the bottom of a pile of half-burnt grass clippings. Is her version of events plausible? I think not. Loretta Shackleton removed Luke's clothes from the scene of the crime and attempted to destroy them. Why? Because she knew damn well that being in possession of the murdered man's clothes could lead to only one conclusion—she killed Luke Bretton. Her testimony is so incredulous and unbelievable for one reason and one reason only—because it is all a pack of lies!

Let's not forget about the victim, Luke. A young man, only twenty-five, his whole life ahead of him. He had a gambling addiction which led him down the path to his demise. Borrowing, stealing, and ultimately—extortion. However, he underestimated the lengths Loretta Shackleton would undergo, to protect her own name and the career of her husband. When you go up against the rich, and powerful then you better be well armed—Luke Bretton wasn't. He was a naïve, troubled young man who was well out of his depth.

His final moments on this earth must have been terrifying. A morbid fear of water. The night of his death the River Wharfe was in full flood—the Strid a furious crucible of hissing water. We can only pray his end was swift and merciful. Killed by the thing he feared the most. Except, it wasn't the River Wharfe which killed him—it was Loretta Shackleton who pushed Luke to his death.

Bernard Ogilvy smiles benevolently at the jury.

'I think the only thing I agree on with my learned friend is there is a lot of information to digest in a murder trial. For it is indeed a murder trial. But is this the murder that never was? Until Eileen Bretton mentioned Luke's phobia, the police were keeping an open mind—homicide, suicide, or misadventure. Is this an example of them becoming so fixated on one aspect of the case they've thrown the baby out with the bathwater?

Let us digest the police investigation and the persons of interest, as Sergeant Stoker called them.

Who had most to gain financially from Luke's death? Katy Kennedy would have inherited half of the house to the value of one hundred and fifty thousand pounds once her mother passed away. How much sweeter to inherit three hundred thousand pounds by getting rid of her despised stepbrother? Did the police think this motive warranted further investigation?

No, they did not.

Dane King was cheated on by his fiancé and best friend, Luke Bretton. Bitter, resentful, and prone to violence. He said in his own words he hated Luke for what he'd done to his life and wished Luke had never been born. Did the police think this motive warranted further investigation?

No, they did not.

Gareth Brady, an old-fashioned loan shark who made sure customers repaid their loans simply by his intimidating physique, looks, and reputation. An ex-boxer with a criminal record for assault and battery. Five thousand in the red to Luke Bretton, but more importantly, a loss of face. If Luke could get away without repaying, then maybe others would follow suit? Did the police think this motive warranted further investigation?

No, they did not.

Miles Brandon, the antique shop owner. The loss of an antique watch stolen by Luke, then threatened if he went to the police, Luke would tell his wife of their sordid relationship. Miles openly admitted he paid Luke for sex. Had Luke begun to blackmail him and did the police think this motive for murder warranted further investigation?

No, they did not.

And lastly, we have Elliot Shackleton. And what was the damning evidence they'd compiled against him? What was the murder-inducing motive they'd discovered? A business card found in Luke's bedroom. Did the police think this evidence warranted further investigation?

Yes, for some bizarre reason, they did.

And yet none of those suspects stand in the dock.

The police did not once question Loretta Shackleton until after she was arrested. Not once was she shown a picture of Luke Bretton. Not once was she asked if she knew him. They have no evidence Loretta Shackleton ever had an affair with Luke Bretton. They have no evidence Loretta Shackleton was being blackmailed by Luke Bretton, but there she stands—accused of murder—maybe the murder that never was...

The prosecution's case has more holes in it than a Swiss cheese factory. If there's even a single shred of doubt in your minds that Loretta Shackleton is Luke Bretton's killer, then you must find her not guilty.'

25

A throng clatters down the staircase from court one. Frank and Zac stare up at the swarm of solicitors, advisors, and bodyguards that encircle Mr and Mrs Shackleton as they descend the steps. Closely behind are a mob of reporters in heightened excitement due to the salacious nature of the story gifted to them on a plate.

'I can't believe it,' Zac murmurs.

Frank wearily sighs. 'When someone blatantly lies on oath, what can you do? The judge didn't help with his summing up and instructions to the jurors. If there's even a sliver of doubt, then they must find the defendant not guilty. He might as well have declared her not guilty himself.'

'Come on, Frank, let's slip out the back away from the press.'

'I wish I could. But Zac, a policeman's lot, is not a happy one. Unfortunately, the Deputy Chief Constable, no less, called me earlier. She said whatever the outcome, I was to front up to the media and act professional.'

Dejected and slightly shellshocked by the day's proceedings, they saunter outside and wait in the wings as Elliot Shackleton addresses the media scrum, his wife by his side.

'I'd like to say my wife and I are obviously delighted and relieved with the verdict. These last six months have been trying, exhausting and, frankly scary. Never for one moment did I doubt my wife. Never for one moment did I doubt in the efficacy of our great judiciary.'

A reporter bustles forward. 'Mr Shackleton, does this mean your political career is back on track? Will you be standing in the next general election?'

Elliot smiles benevolently. 'I have always had the full backing of the party. They have been a great source of comfort to me and my wife. Loretta and I now ask for peace and privacy and a time to reflect. Once we have inwardly digested the calamitous events of the last six months, I will issue a further statement regarding my career. My wife would like to say a few words before we finish up.'

Mrs Shackleton takes a stride forward as cameras click and flash, and boom mics jostle for position. She pulls a sheet of paper from her pocket.

'I have prepared this statement earlier and I won't be taking any further questions. I share the sentiments of my husband. This has been the hardest thing I've ever had to endure and without my husband's unwavering support, I'm not sure I'd have made it through. I would like to offer my sincerest thanks to all my supporters, family, and friends, and especially to Bernard Ogilvy, who bucked me up in times of darkness.

Lastly, I would say this. I bear no malice nor ill-will to the police. Indeed, on the contrary, I am a tremendous supporter of our great police force, and all the men and women who work tirelessly to protect us all. However, sometimes they can get it wrong. That's why we have such a robust and independent judicial system to stop miscarriages of justice. We are all fortunate to live in a country which has such a safeguard, as many other countries do not afford their citizens the same luxury. Thank you.'

A torrent of questions rains forth, but two burly security guards shepherd the Shackleton's down the steps and into a waiting Range Rover. The doors slam as it briskly moves away.

'The sanctimonious, self-serving humility of that was nearly enough to make me puke,' Zac moans.

'Don't take it personally, Zac. Some you win, others you lose,' Frank says as he pulls up his coat collar against a biting wind.

'I let her down,' he says, his voice laced with regret.

'Eileen?'

'Yes. I promised her we'd find Luke's killer.'

'We did Zac, we did,' Frank says as he pats his sergeant on the shoulder. 'Right, time to face the music. Wish me luck.'

'You'll need more than luck with that mob,' Zac replies. 'But good luck anyway, boss.'

'Cheers. We'll find a quiet pub after this and drown our sorrows,' he says as he heads towards the baying media pack. 'Your shout.'

'Funny about that.'

Also By Ely North

DCI Finnegan Yorkshire Crime Thrillers

Book 1: **Black Nab** – Text M For Murder

Book 2: **Jawbone Walk** – Text V For Vengeance

Book 3: **Vertigo Alley** – Text K For Killer

Book 4: **Whitby Toll** – The Bell Rings... But For Whom?

Book 5: **House Arrest** – Escape Can Be A Deadly Road

Book 6: **Gothic Fog** – The Strawman Cometh

Book 7: **Happy Camp** – Discipline, Godliness, Fun!

DCI Finnegan Series Boxset: **Books 1 – 3**

DCI Finnegan Series Boxset: **Books 4 – 6**

Prequel – **Aquaphobia** – The Body in the River (Free ebook for newsletter subscribers)

*Note: All books are available from Amazon in ebook, paperback, and in **Kindle Unlimited** (excluding Aquaphobia). Paperbacks are distributed widely via online retailers (Apple, B&N, Kobo, Amazon etc). **Boxset print editions are one book compiled from three books. They do not come in a box.** *** Pre-orders only apply to ebooks.

Keep In Touch

I hope you enjoyed the opening salvo in the DCI Frank Finnegan, Yorkshire Crime Thriller Series.

This novella was intended as a taster for the rest of the books in the series, of which there will be many.

Below I have included the first six chapters of Book 1 – **BLACK NAB – TEXT M FOR MURDER**. The book is available from **Amazon** now:

Black Nab – Text M For Murder

If you would like to keep up to date with new releases, freebies, and discounts, please join my newsletter, which is designed to entertain. Over the next twelve months, I will be investigating some of the greatest unsolved crimes from that last 120 years; posting reviews and recommendations on the latest crime fiction I have read; and sharing insights as to how I come up with characters and plot lines and stitch them all together in the writing process. If it sounds like fun, sign up today – you can unsubscribe at any time.

SIGN ME UP TO YOUR NEWSLETTER

If you are reading in paperback, then please just drop me a line via email and I'll manually add you to my list.

ely@elynorthcrimefiction.com

Printed in Great Britain
by Amazon

41437957R00091